A Delightful Impropriety

Lady Jane knew that having Lord Alex come to her studio to view her portrait of him was not entirely proper. But only now did she realize how dangerous it might be.

Jane found herself rocking on her heels, taken by surprise, unable to believe she was actually in Alex's arms. He was gentle with her, kissing her far more lightly than he might have, and releasing her though she made no struggle, but even that was enough to make her respond like a flower to the sun.

He smiled at her and said, "Tomorrow I shall send my valet for your painting."

With that, he departed, and Jane returned to the portrait, still on its easel. She ran her fingertips over his lips, and they seemed to come alive under her touch. *What am I doing?* she wondered. *What is happening to me?*

The beating of her heart, the pulsing of her blood, gave her an answer she could not deny. . . .

The Elusive Rake

Marcy Elias Rothman

A SIGNET BOOK

SIGNET
Published by the Penguin Group
Penguin Books USA Inc., 375 Hudson Street,
New York, New York 10014, U.S.A.
Penguin Books Ltd, 27 Wrights Lane,
London W8 5TZ, England
Penguin Books Australia Ltd,
Ringwood, Victoria, Australia
Penguin Books Canada Ltd, 10 Alcorn Avenue,
Toronto, Ontario, Canada M4V 3B2
Penguin Books (N.Z.) Ltd, 182–190 Wairau Road,
Auckland 10, New Zealand

Penguin Books Ltd, Registered Offices:
Harmondsworth, Middlesex, England

First published by Signet, an imprint of Dutton Signet,
a division of Penguin Books USA Inc.

First Printing, March, 1997
10 9 8 7 6 5 4 3 2 1

This book was written with the generosity of friends and experts who willingly shared their hard-won insights with me.

I thank you with all my heart:

Kay Dangaard, of Los Angeles; Carol and Jesse Vogel; Dena Katz; Wylma Wayne, my London claque; and artist friends, Evelyn Glaubman and Sharon Dabney of California.

Katherine Coombs, Curatorial Assistant in Prints and Paintings, Victoria and Albert Museum, London, and her associates, Sara Heming and Daniel Parker; and Scot Levitt, V.P., Butterfield and Butterfield, Los Angeles, lent their valuable time to me as well.

Prologue

Ireland, Daitry Hall, 1815

Lady Jane Daitry moved quickly to find the closest and most advantageous view of the dining room before the evening light failed. Luckily she had long sight and soon finding a suitable perch, she lifted her skirts and fell to her knees. She took out a drawing pad and with long, tapering fingers captured in lightning strokes the well-shaped head, capped by wavy blond hair and the fined-boned face, now interested, now briefly animated, thoughtful, always distant and aloof.

The head belonged to Alexander Barrington. To her regret, Jane had gone from abject hero worship of her brother's rescuer to intense dislike in the space of a fortnight. He made her feel a nonentity in her own home. Jane laughed ruefully, honesty compelling her to admit she probably deserved to be overlooked by this startlingly handsome London paragon.

Knowing herself to be too shy and never socially secure, Jane knew better than anyone she would never be the belle of the ball. At twenty-six, with her ungainly height, unruly black Irish mane, and pale complexion, she had long since given up any lingering ambition to be an integral part of Craig Bay society or hope of being a devastating charmer. Her party manners were deplorable, or so her brother said, and she had no interest in anything that didn't revolve around her painting. And worse, she had no flair for the female wiles she

had read about. Indeed, she deserved to be overlooked.
How could she expect anything more? She was, consid-
ering the state and coffers of Daitry Hall, below the
touch of such a rich London nonpareil and one so high
in the instep as the fourth Earl of Trent. Yet for all that,
he came to life at the end of her drawing pencil.

No matter. Alex Barrington had his uses. As artistic
fodder, Barrington was ideal and, after all, what else
really interested or drove her? The man had a head so
magnificent she itched to paint him in every mood. The
pile of sketches grew at her side, while her fingers flew
over the pages. How often did she have a chance to
work with anyone so perfect? She discarded everything from her mind to concentrate on the drawings.

As satisfied as she would ever be, Jane worked until
the light faded. Finally recalling the time, she reluctantly bundled her papers and charcoals into a large
reticule, raced down through a small stand of trees,
and entered the great hall of Daitry Hall by a side door.
Her brother and his companion were just leaving the
dining room to join her in the drawing room. Jane had
timed it to a nicety.

She slipped into the room seconds before their arrival and took her place at the piano, idly strumming
along the keyboard, afraid to look up and catch the eye
of the man who had saved her brother's life, but who
now, damn his blue-gray eyes, treated Patrick's
homage with disdain.

It would not do for Alexander Barrington, the man
whose head and body she had secretly memorialized
over the past week in dozens of studies, to know how
she felt about him or what she was doing. He was a
very disturbing man to be around, and the sooner he
left, the better.

It was bad enough that he ignored her. She could understand that. But to treat her sweet, loving Patrick like
some annoying gnat, an importuning acolyte, made
her blood boil.

She wanted him out of the house, and she wanted it now. As long as Barrington stayed in Ireland, she could not embark on a program to bring Patrick back to health.

Jane's fingers thundered along the keyboard in harmony with her rising anger and frustration. Life had not thrown any genuine heroes and London swells in her midst, and to go from slavish devotion to a man to sheer hatred was too much to be comfortable.

Suddenly Alexander Barrington turned toward her and frowned.

Jane was secretly pleased, and assailed the keys even harder. She felt a small triumph, even if she very nearly broke the poor old piano in the process. At last she had succeeded in attaching his attention.

Barrington rose with the most infuriating languid motion and strolled over to the piano bench, where without a word he followed her lead across the keyboard. His powerful fingers, his touch, his musicianship were a world away from Jane's country skill. She stopped playing and moved away, tears gathering in her eyes.

She would never forgive him for showing her the depths of her inferiority. She shuddered to think what he would say if he saw her sketches and paintings. She might be able to live with an attack on her musicianship, for that was a mere diversion she held little store by, but if he attacked her work, she would be wounded irretrievably. Few people knew she had aspirations, that she wanted to become a major artist. How or when didn't matter.

She would never forget nor forgive Alexander Barrington for spoiling Patrick's homecoming for her.

She hated his assumption of natural superiority. She hated the Earl of Trent, and always would, and, thankfully, once he left she would never have to see him again.

Chapter One

Ireland, February, 1818

Her face mottled, small dark eyes bulging with the righteous anger she could summon like a summer storm, Verna Daitry, the Countess of Daitry, picked up Jane's sketchbook and charcoals and flung them with all her might across the black-and-white marble tiles of the entry hall.

"The larder and the port need watching from the thieving servants and the sheets need mending, but does that bother you?" she cried out, proceeding to answer her own question. "No. You and that precious husband of mine are too good to shivvy the servants' backsides from their tea the whole day long. A shiftless lot they are, and no mistake."

Unbelieving, Lady Jane Daitry watched her work skitter along the ground, crashing, in turn, against the old Celtic chest near the wide, double-glass doors. They looked like flotsam after a shipwreck, and indeed they were not far from a symbol of the wreckage of her life. They were among the most prized of all her meager possessions and the few things that had enabled her to endure the last two years. In truth, the drawing materials bought with her meager allowance had been her chief consolation for more than half her life, and seeing them broken and scattered this way made her want to scream and wreak havoc on Verna.

Shock and rage battled in her head, but she held on,

if not for her own sake, then for Patrick's. It didn't do to get Verna angry. It didn't do at all. Jane and her brother were notoriously susceptible to Verna's voice which could rise like thunder and shake the rafters. Years of her parents banging doors, long, hateful silences, silent tears, and sick headaches, were different, and decidedly preferable to Verna's confrontational ways.

"Are you deef like that brother of yours when it suits him to drive me mad?" Verna, nee Bridie Byrne, asked her sister-in-law bitterly. Verna might now choose a more refined first name, but her language and speech unfortunately retained her origins as a babe in an Irish bog and later a social outcast among the Brahmins of Boston.

"Deaf, Verna, deaf," Jane Daitry said reflexively, her voice barely more than a murmur. Actually, between them she and Patrick preferred to call it domestic deafness. To say anything more, to reveal her true feelings toward this harridan was too horrible to contemplate, and Jane wanted nothing more than to shut her ears and go away and hide. It was what she usually did when Verna was on the march, as she was today.

If it weren't for poor Patrick, Jane would have long since smashed the pudding face and the voice that could shatter glass. Verna had been terrorizing and spoiling everything she and her brother Patrick believed made life worth living. Jane was fast becoming unable to tolerate the woman's practiced, petty tyrannies. Nothing could stop Verna and her increasingly wild outbursts. Challenging her only exacerbated matters, not so much for herself, but for poor Patrick, who had no way of removing himself from the situation. She, at least, had her love of the house, her paints, her music, and the horses.

"If you must paint, for Gawd's sake, paint the saints," Verna hissed, mounting one of her special hobby horses. "No. you must drive me mad painting this miserable rundown wreck of a house and everyone who comes in sight of you."

"The saints have been well served by da Vinci and Michelangelo and don't need my poor efforts," Jane said. She was too worn down to continue the same old useless arguments. "I haven't the nerve or the talent for religious art. Yet I am surprised you ask. You have told me often enough I paint like a child."

"Paint dishes, if you must paint something. We could use another set, the Lord knows, the others have chips enough to cut a body's mouth" Verna's disdain flitted to another favorite subject.

Jane could tell Verna was still spoiling for a fight. The signs were there for anyone to see. Her cheeks were redder than ever, her breathing ragged, big hands kneading her ample hips. Patrick always said Verna loved a fight better than a hot meal and grew a foot when she prevailed in an argument with brother or sister, which seemed to happen with great frequency lately.

It was no surprise really, Daitrys weren't bred for arguments, and were at a sore disadvantage in Verna's prized forum. She was a master at uncovering a person's weaknesses and battering at them. It seemed to Jane that Verna had raised this talent to an art. And now a real brannigan was brewing, and Jane didn't know how to stop it from happening. She hated the ugliness of it all and shut her mind more firmly than ever against Verna's latest tirade.

"If you'll excuse me, I will see to the linen," Jane said quietly, walking toward the debris made by her drawings and charcoals. She knew she hadn't a hope of deflecting Verna's ire, but she had to try.

Verna put her hand out to stop her.

"Leave that mess, and damn the linen. I want to talk to you."

A new sound entered Verna's voice. Though hard to imagine, it seemed to strike a conciliatory note.

"What about?" Jane tensed, instantly on the alert.

"Come sit down by me," Verna said, pointing to two large wing chairs set in a niche below the stairs at the back of the hall.

"Verna, I really haven't time to stop," Jane said firmly. The prospect of Verna, the confidante, was worse than Verna, the ogress. Afraid of what was coming, Jane maneuvered so that she was in the middle of the hall, her favorite place in the rambling house. Standing on a large star imbedded in the marble floor, there was the wonderful promise of the most spectacular views of the four sides of the house. No matter what the provocation that drove her to the spot, the view of Craig Bay ahead, woodland behind, parkland to the west, and lush gardens to the east, gave Jane's mind a measure of artistic ease, even if her mind was in turmoil this late-winter morning.

From the time she was a child, Jane blessed the genius of the man who had designed Daitry Hall one hundred years earlier. He must have been more than an architect, she thought, more like an artist with an eye for some of the most spectacular vistas in all of Ireland. As a child Jane had discovered that by standing on the star encircled in the middle of the entry hall, the floor-to-ceiling windows and glass front doors gave an unrestricted access to the breathtaking scenes in every direction.

It was here that Jane could be found at dawn or dusk, drawing endlessly, and it was here that Verna had cornered her today.

"Come sit down, Jane dear," Verna said, renewing her invitation.

"Can't we talk here?"

"Have it your own way," Verna said shortly, assuming what Jane called her sister-in-law's magisterial look, and at last joined her in the middle of the hall. "I have given permission for Mr. Jameson to pay his addresses to you. He will offer for you at tea tomorrow. Now do you want to sit down?"

Jane stared, sure she had misheard.

"You didn't say what I thought you said?" Jane asked, trying to keep her voice from rising in hysteria.

"Don't play the innocent with me," Verna stated firmly. "It's time you married, and Jameson is as good as anyone."

Jane stared in horror. Joseph Jameson was a man twice her age, with hands like hams, thighs like tree trunks, and a face red from exploring the dregs of port in his glass every night.

"He'll cure you of your everlasting stoopid pictures."

Jane stopped in her tracks. Why did everything always come down to her paintings? Some of the steam seeped out of her anger. It had driven her mother wild, and had drawn sarcasm from her father, who called it her English affectation. No one wanted to understand that drawing was the only release she had from the endless conflicts and isolation. The Daitrys' increasing poverty prevented them from entertaining, and she had no friends her own age. They were very nearly outcasts, and if she hadn't discovered her small talent, God knows what would have happened to her.

Only Patrick was understanding about her art, when he was home. Live and let live was her brother's way of handling any unpleasantness. She loved him for and in spite of his weaknesses. It had always been so.

And then Verna had come along and had seized on her painting as an easy bone to gnaw at. She was well aware that her sister-in-law hated the marked differences in their social status and appearance. Where she was tall and had thick, black hair and blue eyes, Verna was short and given to a heavy middle and thin, wiry hair.

Jane shook her head, suddenly realizing that Joseph Jameson would soon be lost in the argument between them.

"Tell me, Verna, why didn't you marry Joseph?" Jane asked mildly.

Verna shrugged, but not before Jane could see it was an unwelcome question.

"Talk was that you and Joseph had an understanding, but that was before Patrick came home from Waterloo, wasn't it?" Jane asked shrewdly, guessing from the embarrassment on Verna's face she was right.

"He wasn't good enough after you had set your cap for my brother, but he's good enough for me. Is that the truth?"

"It's time you were marrying and leaving this hole," Verna pressed on. "This pathetic attachment of yours to the house is a joke." A dig about its decrepitude was always good for a rise out of her, Jane thought.

"How strange. Early on, when you came to tea, you said the house was perfection, the dishes worthy of the Regent's own table. And my paintings? A lost genius in the wilds of Ireland, you said," Jane mimicked sweetly, trying to get a little of her own back, something she seldom bothered to do.

"Tell the truth and shame the devil," Verna said, her voice softening greatly. "'You're fallin' for the blue eyes and the bloody title, stupid girl,' Pa said. And he was right. I loved and still love Patrick with all my heart."

Jane smiled. She had watched Verna's campaign to snare her brother. His crippled legs and the decay of the estate might discourage other women, but not Verna. Besides, it was her only chance to become a member of the gentry, and she seized on it fiercely. Jane still wanted to believe that eventually Verna would learn to control her sulfuric temper and become less outspoken.

Yet the very least Jane owed her sister-in-law and herself was a little honest recollection of history.

"You married Patrick with your eyes wide open." Jane said. It was useless, but human, she decided, to remind Verna of the concerted efforts she and her father had waged to snare Patrick into a marriage he didn't want.

Whatever consequences followed were predictable. Hadn't Jane tried to tell her brother what he was letting himself in for?

"Jane, I am at my wit's end," he had pleaded with her for understanding hours on end before the marriage. "Mama's money ran out years ago on Papa's slow horses and high living. He lived the life of a country gentleman on tick for years, and this is the result. We are broke and need Mike Byrne's money to restore the place, for let's face it, no one else wants to marry me."

Again, Verna brought Jane back to the discussion at hand.

"Never mind all that old history," Verna said, recovering herself. "The fact remains the estate needs an infusion of new money. Everything's mortgaged to the ears, and no one is knocking your door down with a better offer than Joe Jameson. Take him and be done with it. Sometimes I think me father was right. He says we should tear down the old pile and be rid of it. I told him over me dead body."

Jane didn't for a moment question that Big Mike Byrne had said just that. He was certainly right about all the reasons Verna had chosen Patrick for a husband. After all, he didn't make a fortune in the building trade in America by being stupid.

However, what neither family had taken into account after the marriage was the depth of ostracism they would all suffer at the hands of the local gentry.

"Darling Jane, if only Verna weren't so difficult, " Mrs. Muir, the vicar's wife, herself blunt to a fault, told Jane after a particularly difficult party, at which Verna had drunk too much.

Jane tried to explain.

"Verna is not a bad woman, but she is impatient and from her upbringing tends to think she knows best. I admire her in many ways for her unbridled honesty."

But the last straw was Verna's performance at the most popular public fete, a summer fair. Verna had criticized everything in sight and had torn into the chief social lionesses of the county in full sight and sound of their tenants and anyone of importance for twenty miles around. Verna's performance put an end to her vaulting social ambitions and began the isolation of the family. Verna went to bed for a week and apologized abjectly, but their isolation continued.

"Blast it, you are daydreaming again," Verna lashed out.

"I'm sorry, Verna. What were you saying?"

Jane knew at once she had made a bad mistake admitting that she hadn't been attending. Of, course it threw Verna into one of her more virulent rages.

Wildly looking around for something to vent her spleen on, Verna's attention was drawn to Jane's ancient paint box, patched and held together by wire and prayer. Jane saw the direction Verna was taking and watched her walk to the box hidden nearby.

"Please don't," Jane cried out.

"You witch." It was the voice of Patrick Daitry, his wheelchair careening toward his wife, sending her crying quietly to a corner.

"No. Patrick. No." Jane turned and ran to him as he moved toward his wife. "It doesn't matter. It really doesn't."

"Patrick, darlin', I wouldn't have thrown the box," Verna cried. "She just got me mad. You know I'm just a bag of wind."

Patrick stopped, breathing heavily, and looked at his sister and then at his wife. He fell back in his chair, almost tipping it over, and then left the hall.

Patrick was still breathing fire when he reached the stables.

"Ready the pony cart for me, and quickly," he ordered Chick Murphy, a scruffy-looking stable hand, one of the new staff Verna had hired over his futile objections. She hired and fired with the regularity of a metronome.

Patrick propelled the cart and pony out of the stables and onto the road parallel to Craig Bay allowing his anger to dissipate, until he realized he had no place to go. Verna had seen to that. Doors of his friends and neighbors were open to him and Jane, but not to Verna. For good or bad, she was his countess, and he had to stand by her. He drove aimlessly, cursing himself for being so blind to Jane's misery and the long tyranny she was subjected to by Verna. The truth of the matter was that Jane never complained, and he didn't often see or want to see what needed his concern.

He looked down at the plaid rug spread across his withered legs and the crutches he used only when he left the house.

Alex Barrington had not done him a great service extricating him from under his horse in the final cavalry charge at Waterloo. And what the hell had Patrick been doing there in the first place, when he should have been home taking over the estate and caring for Jane? He should have been in Ireland picking up the pieces and, yes, marrying rich, and seeing to Jane's future. She never reminded him of his selfishness and his responsibilities toward her. He probably wouldn't have listened anyway. Jane had her paints, the piano, and the horses, and seemed content. He chose to believe she was happy because it suited him, his conscience reminded him.

Where were his eyes all those years, dawdling as an aide to a general at the War Office who waged his war in the drawing rooms of London? He had a marvelous time dancing attendance wherever young officers were welcome, which was everywhere, and begging for a chance to fight the resurgent Napoleon. Thus when the chance to see combat finally arose, it was too good to miss.

Patrick groaned aloud. A mild rain, no more than a mist, made him think about shelter. The nearest house belonged to Madge Brooks, and he headed there.

Of all the people Verna had managed to alienate, Aunt Madge was the only one who still came to tea at Dairy Hall and infrequently had all the Daitrys to dine. It was tacitly understood that there were never other guests on those occasions.

Madge Brooks was a girlhood friend of Patrick's mother. During their first season in London, the two lovely young women of good English families fell madly in love with two Irish friends who were hunting for rich wives. The two couples married after whirlwind courtships and moved together to Ireland.

There the women led far different lives from what they had expected. Mary Daitry produced two children and watched, heavy-hearted, as Thomas Daitry squandered her fortune and bedded any woman who took his fancy. In contrast, loving Frank Brooks increased Madge's fortune. The one mar to their lives was never having children.

With no family to speak of in Ireland or England, Madge Brooks was the closest thing to a real aunt that the Daitry sister and brother had. And when their mother suffered one of her "spells," Madge had been often a mother to them as well.

Gray-haired, small, and dumpy, her beautiful dresses, made by an expensive modiste in London, were always simple and elegant. Outspoken, Madge was also shrewd and perceptive. On this wet evening she greeted Patrick, with all the warmth he could wish for, ordered her butler to take Patrick's soaking hacking jacket to be dried and to bring one of her husband's old dressing gowns.

The sight of the man she loved like a son shuffling into her drawing room on his cursed crutches, his face grayer and more worn than usual, moved her to tears, and she withdrew to the fireplace.

She knew the life of quiet desperation he and Jane lived at Daitry Hall, and her heart went out to them. It was hardly a surprise that Verna had turned out to be a horror. For weeks she had joined Jane in pleading with Patrick not to marry Verna, but they were never able to budge him. In that respect Patrick was —much as she loved this tall, dark-haired, once strong-as-an-oak young man—given to going his own stubborn way, much like his father.

"Aunt Madge, I'm at my wit's end," Patrick said without preamble, sitting on a couch facing her, everything about him a picture of utter dejection. He told her all he had witnessed at the house and of the years of unremitting struggle. "I am determined that Jane get away for a while."

Madge listened carefully, urging more tea and scones on him. He was much too thin and fragile-looking.

"You know, this means you and Verna will be alone," Mrs. Brooks noted, watching Patrick closely. She was forcing him to think deeply about what he was proposing. The affection between Jane and Patrick was one of the most moving things about them. Everyone said so. She knew Patrick would be lost without Jane to buffer his misery.

"I'm just beginning to understand how selfish I have been. I may have ruined Jane's life."

Madge smiled to herself.

"Don't take it all on yourself, dear boy," she said, deciding it was about time Patrick grew up and learned a few home truths. "Your parents started the process. When Jane was eighteen I begged your mother to let me sponsor a season for her in London and arrange for her to have art lessons. She refused, saying she needed Jane to run the house and stand as buffer to your father."

Patrick put down his cup and saucer. His face colored. To her children, Lady Mary Daitry was a walking or, more accurately, a recumbent saint, smothered in gauze in a darkened room for most of their lives.

"I can hardly believe it."

"Yes, you do, Patrick," Madge Brooks said coolly. "I blame myself that I didn't push hard enough to give Jane a London season. She's fast becoming an old maid. But listen closely."

With wide, broad strokes she told Patrick how she planned to ask Jane to accompany her to London for the season.

"I will get her married, if it's the last thing I do," she said finally, warming to her plans.

Patrick suddenly felt a terrible burden lift from his shoulders.

Jane was going to have a wonderful time in London, and a husband at the end of it.

He left Madge's house whistling.

Chapter Two

London 1819

"**Y**ou're out of your mind," Alexander Barrington howled, wrestling with the heavy rumpled coverlet.

"Darling, listen," Clea Wesley laughed, long, voluptuously rounded arms moving in the air in an effort to coax him back to bed. "Marriage isn't so bad, if you manage it properly."

Barrington howled louder. "I will not be embroiled in one of your mad schemes, and that's the end of it," He protested, even as he avoided her arms.

He was bent on making a hasty exit from this female predator, and he meant to do it with as much clothing as he could collect. It simply wouldn't do for the neighbors in this quiet byway where their love nest was located to see him in such disarray. It didn't matter a tinker's damn to Clea what their neighbors thought, but strangely it bothered Alex. He certainly didn't mind what his own highborn friends and the residents saw of his rowdy existence in Portman Square. But here it was different.

In truth, he loved to shock the *ton*, and did so as often as possible. But in his experience many of the doctors and barristers who were their neighbors watched over the sensibilities of their wives and children far more than most of his society friends. He respected their feelings, even if Clea did not.

Alex continued to clomp around the bedroom, trying to shut out Clea's siren song. He was not going back to bed, even though it was exactly what he wanted to do, but he needed to be deaf to her pleas. Clea was a diverting mistress, an exciting companion, up to every foolish prank, who loved to tweak her nose at convention as much as he did, but when she took it into her gorgeous head to be bloody-minded, she was a force of nature.

"Where are my trews, damn it?" Alex demanded, his impatience hampering the hunt.

"You fool" Clea laughed gleefully, lighting a candle to the accompaniment of a prodigious and unbroken string of army oaths issuing from various parts of the room.

"You might help me, you witch," Alex started to say, but thought better of it. "Never mind. I know your help. My clothes will be out the window in a wink."

She made a motion to quit the bed. To someone like Clea, who never spurned a challenge, the idea was too delicious to let pass.

"Don't even think of it," Alex warned, unsure whether she would listen to him. He would ring her neck if she tried depositing his clothes out the window.

At last he found his boots, his inexpressibles eluding him. He was getting even more angry as he imagined the sight he made stomping around the bedroom at dusk desperately looking for his shirt and drawers.

Even so he loved hearing her laughter. It often surprised him that they could still have such an interest in each other. It was a record for him. No other woman had ever held his attention for so long. Neither pretended to be faithful to the other, but still they returned refreshed and ravenous for the other's talents between the sheets.

It was two years since he and Clea had first made love. He expected he would have had enough of her, and in many ways he was beginning to. But she was still the most inventive woman he had ever made love with, and her outrageousness gave him one of the few reasons he had to smile these days.

Coming across a heap of satin and chambray that Clea had discarded hastily hours before, made him chuckle.

But there were limits even to his amusement and tolerance of her intrigues, and Clea had just reached the danger point. It was perfectly permissible for her to come up with one of her mad schemes for others, but not for him. And Clea's latest suggestion really frightened him.

"Think on it, Alex," Clea said sweetly. "In one stroke we would resolve all our dilemmas."

"Your family dilemmas, not mine, dear Clea," he reminded her.

Clea's terrible suggestion that he marry because her husband wanted to be a prime minister and her daughter wanted to marry an heir to a dukedom was the Wesley family problem and no concern of his. That Clea's husband was demanding his wife be more discreet in her affair with him in order to further these new ambitions was all well and good, but not at the price of Alexander Barrington's prized freedom. There was no way at all he was going to be leg-shackled to anyone. No way at all.

By now Alex's search brought him dangerously close to the bed, and Clea leaned over the side trying to snare him. He escaped her grasp, as he always did.

"Will you at least give Mabel some thought?" Clea asked with some hope in her voice.

"As far as I am concerned, marriage is for securing the line, and my brother Edward, whom I love with all my heart, has three sturdy sons and has more than adequately taken care of that small detail for me."

"But you don't even know the girl I have my heart

set on for you. She is lovely and very pliable. You know I would make certain you would suit. We could go on as we are and people would stop talking about us."

Indeed, he wasn't acquainted with Mable Seymour, and that was the way he intended things to remain. With Clea's Machiavellian mind, Alex knew Mabel might be an angel, but only to her parents. Furthermore he didn't give a damn for society. Alex was trying to manage the conversation and his search for his clothes with detachment, but the whole matter was turning into a French farce, and that he didn't like at all.

Just at the point he decided to call a servant or order Clea to help, Alex noticed his trews peaking out from under a chair near the bed. He made a dash for them and, hopping around like a stork with tail feathers afire, got the wrong leg in, lost his footing, and catapulted back into Clea's arms.

"What the hell," Alex laughed as he reached for her. Her family problems could wait another time.

Exultant, Clea clung to him for as long as she could. She was too shrewd not to suspect that her days as Alex's mistress were numbered if she didn't do something drastic. But for the moment he was still hers, and she intended not to lose a second of the pleasure he gave her.

Chapter Three

Patrick Daitry's return journey to Daitry Hall was in stunning contrast to his departure hours before.

The pony fairly flew through the warm, redolent dusk. Sheep gamboled among the outcroppings on the hills, and in the deep valley, fields were covered with a kind of velvet green man could never replicate. After the rain, the air was clean, smelling a little of peat, and the sky was blue and cloudless.

He was going home to do something he should have done years ago, and his heart fairly sung with the prospect of the good he would do. Patrick gave the pony her head and went over some of the things he and Aunt Madge had decided between them.

"I need you to supply me with at list of eligible gentlemen who can be relied on to squire Jane around London and introduce her to important people, if they do not become enamored of her themselves," she insisted. " I must have some prospects to go on with. My brother is a recluse, and my circle is all old ladies like myself."

"I wouldn't want most of the fellows I knew to meet Jane," he'd replied. He was adamant about that. His old army comrades who were still unmarried were a ramshackle set who would not take to Jane at all. She was too much the bluestocking for them.

"I'm afraid, dear Patrick, I need a starting point," she had insisted. "Think on it."

"The only man I know with the stature you will need

to make a fine splash with Jane is the Earl of Trent," he had finally confessed. "He saved my life, but he is a famous curmudgeon, and would rake me up one side and down the other if I dared land him with my uncompromising sister."

Patrick loved Jane more than anyone in the world, and knew he would be doing his sister a great disservice to allow her to meet the earl again. The man was a satyr with a terrible temper and Jane was far below his touch socially.

"It would be an unmitigated disaster involving Alexander Barrington," Patrick said. "He very nearly got himself killed rescuing me and forbade me to speak of it around the regiment on pain of a lashing."

"Barrington will never do," Madge Brooks agreed at once. "He is too notorious for a decent woman to know."

However this last didn't stop her engaging in a good gossip. She poured a drink for Patrick and happily indulged herself in a long coze on the affair between Clea Wesley and Alexander Barrington.

"No! I would prefer more eligible escorts for Jane," she went on. "Besides, Clea has him tied like a hog."

Asking his one-time commanding officer for a favor might go against the grain, but was not to be dismissed so easily. He owed Madge Brooks all the aid he could give her, and what she was offering Jane was a damned sight more than he could afford with Verna's endless cheese paring.

Other men might expect to control their wives' fortunes, but Verna's father and his lawyers had run circles around Patrick's country solicitor. The old lawyer had begged him to hire a Dublin man to deal with Mike Byrne and his people, but at that point Patrick was so disgusted with the whole matter, he had told his man to conclude the negotiations as quickly as possible.

Patrick knew he had set his sights too low. All he had wanted was enough money to set the estate to rights and provide a proper setting for Jane to shine before the local county families with marriageable sons, though there were precious few of them. He owed Jane that, for there had been few women of fortune and birth who considered him proper marriage material, with his bad leg and ruined lands. The only one he had formed a *tendre* for was Deidre Mahon, and she had lost no time turning him down in no uncertain and cruel terms.

"You're not the Adonis you were before Waterloo, Pat Daitry," she had told him, compounding the insult. "And don't think anyone else will have you. You're not only crippled, but you're sullen with it, and poor as dirt."

It was then that Verna had appeared on the scene with her barely disguised intention of marrying him. If not precisely heaven-sent, at least she proved a momentary sop to his wounded pride. When she invited him to take her on a picnic and made no secret she wanted him to make love to her, Patrick obliged. It had been a thoroughly satisfying roll on the floor in a nearby empty cottage.

Verna proved far from a blushing virgin, and in subsequent tumbles in the haylofts about the estate, she had taught Patrick a few pointers. Abstinent for so long, he was an apt pupil. The wedding banns were posted; Verna was with child, and the matter settled.

The honeymoon was nothing short of a disaster. There was no baby, and so much for a man's getting hold of his wife's fortune after the wedding bells pealed. Verna's money was tied up like baled hay. What Patrick had to spend on Daitry Hall was what Verna and her father thought necessary, and between them they begrudged him every penny he could beg out of them.

*   *   *

Jane was standing in the road between Craig Bay and the house, her face set in worry lines, searching, in every direction for signs of Patrick. She had gone looking for him after his untimely witness to her argument with his wife. The murderous look on his face frightened Verna as well as Jane, and the two had made temporary peace.

The sound of the pony and cart borne on an errant breeze over the bay made Jane take a deep breath of relief, the first in hours.

She waved until Patrick noticed her and slowed the pony. Jane lifted her riding skirts and with long, graceful steps ran to the cart, swinging easily into the seat, and hugged him in pure joy. He rumpled her curly, black hair, and they rode back to the house.

Under easy banter, Patrick studied Jane's magnificent dark blue eyes. Once bright and alive to adventure and deviltry, they were now quiet, too thoughtful for his peace of mind.

At Eton, Sandhurst, and later in the army, he thought his Jane a happy child, particularly when mounted on any horse at hand, riding around the estate free as air. If only she had complained of the secondhand life she led with their parents, he might have come home to rescue her, or so he wanted to believe.

"Aunt Madge says you were Mama's handmaiden all the years I was away," Patrick said, his eyes staring straight ahead. He didn't want to see the expression on Jane's face.

"Madge exaggerates, love." Jane placed her gloved hand on his slim wrist. She didn't want to stir up old history, especially after the scene with Verna. She and he were trapped, with no way out for either of them. Marry Jameson? The thought chilled her to the bone.

"I feel a ranking bastard for having left you here to face things alone."

Jane smiled. Bitterness would get neither of them anywhere. It wasn't often Jane allowed herself to think about the terrible argument between her mother and Aunt Madge when she was eighteen. She wasn't supposed to know, but she had heard her godmother plead for permission to give her a proper London comeout, along with her mother's refusal without explanation.

"I had my painting, my books, and Mama's piano," Jane said, and indeed they were still everything to her.

"And now you are handmaiden to Verna," Patrick said fiercely.

Jane bit her lip. Patrick saw her do it and knew it to be a sure sign she had her own demons. The small gesture reminded him of their childhood when they hadn't the courage to stand up to their father in any of his drunken tirades. Jane had soothed him then, as she did now.

"Well, that's all over. You are going to be free." He hoped he sounded more convincing than he felt for he didn't have a clue how he would bend Verna to his will. But he would get the money for Jane to go to London somehow.

His wife was the most formidable woman he had ever met. He had learned that on his honeymoon when she admitted she had lied to him about the baby. It was the only way, she said, to force him into marrying her. By then he had lost his courage. The deed was done. Verna had his name.

"You are making Verna a virago by default," his sister told him months after the wedding. "In her way she loves you, and you should try to change her by slow degrees. If you allow her to dominate you, she will be spoiled forever."

Of course, he hadn't listened. What could an unmarried, naive girl like his sister know about the things that went on between a man and his wife? And now the both of them lived with the terror of Verna's mercurial temper and dissatisfaction with everything.

They rode on until they reached the derelict stables, where Verna waited for them. Patrick gave the horse and cart to a stable hand, and got down to the cobbles as best he could.

"Where did you run off to?" Verna asked him in a snide tone of voice.

"I would like both of you to meet me in the library."

What followed was an hour none of the three would ever forget. Patrick poured them all brandy and ordered them to take seats.

"Jane, you are going to London with Aunt Madge, and you, Verna, are going to foot the bill."

"Over me dead body."

"If necessary," Patrick said, enjoying his first experience of renewed manhood in two years.

Jane left the couch. Much as she wanted to go to London, she would not go as an unpaid companion-cum-servant to Aunt Madge, or anyone else. She would slit her throat rather than know that whatever pleasure was in store would be reluctantly paid for by her sister-in-law and out of her brother's hide.

Watching Patrick assert himself was a heady thing, but she didn't want to be the cause of further division between him and Verna.

"Has anyone inquired as to how I feel about all this?" Jane asked, all at once disgusted with a everyone. "You discuss me with Madge Brooks and your wife like I'm some prized horse you are haggling over. I won't have it. It's too late for me anyway."

"You don't understand," Patrick pleaded. He should have known how much she would resent being the last to know what he and Madge had planned for her. God help them if she knew all the secret machinations going forward to find her a husband and a new life in London.

"It's a good thing you're being missish, God-all-mighty Jane Daitry, 'cause you'll not see a penny of my money, and that's a fact."

"Jane, would you leave us alone, please." Matters were getting out of hand. His head was splitting. Instead of kissing him and thanking him for trying to rewrite history, his sister was being difficult, his wife impossible. He couldn't do anything right it seemed. He wished himself a mile away.

Jane stood up and walked out of the room, across the heroically sized center hall, and stopping above the star in the center. There she pivoted on one foot, so she could see the great views on all four sides surrounding the house. Tears rolled down her face, blinding the steep climb to her room. It seemed to take an eternity to reach the only sanctum she had.

She been handed a gift of a lifetime, and booted it away like some child who didn't get the pudding she wanted. No one understood better than she the genesis of Patrick's sudden impulse to right all the wrongs that had kept her rooted to her parents' side, the house, and Ireland. If she had only given in to Verna earlier in the day, all would have been relatively peaceful in the house, or as much at peace as was possible. But instead she had taunted Verna, and look what had happened.

There was a time when the chance to go to London, to be presented at court, to dance the night away, to go to the opera, the theater, libraries, and, most of all, to see all the art that the capital offered an aspiring artist would have meant the world to her. But not anymore. Her enthusiasm for London and its treasures were long gone. It didn't do to expect too much of life.

At twenty-six, Jane felt older than the quiet waters of Craig Bay beyond her windows. Reasonably content most of the time, it was too late for silent aspirations and private desires. She had loved solitude and the comfort of the house, at least until Verna had came to make her life one long battle. She tried to be loving, tried to make a friend of her sister-in-law and ease her into the gentry, but clearly she had not succeeded.

Jane threw herself on the bed and beat her strong, chapped hands, crayon-, and paint-smudged, on the worn-out counterpane. Why had Patrick gone to Aunt Madge and given her new hope of heaven? No one ever knew how much she had yearned for London in the barren years. But what good would it have done her to lament? She was tired, too afraid to dream that London would be anything but disappointing in every way. Don't hope, you fool, she cautioned herself, nothing will come of Patrick's foolishness.

The battle in the library must have been titanic. Jane could hear the raised voices. She put her hands over her ears to block it all out.

"Verna, I will not ask you again," Patrick shouted, his hands in an iron grip around a heavily edged brandy glass, his third drink since Jane had left them. "I'll sell land if you don't release enough money for Jane to go to London in style."

Patrick knew it was a threat that would break his heart if he had to follow through on it. Times were bad and land cheap. He felt about land as Jane felt about her drawings and paintings. The estate was in his blood. But the more Verna pushed him to the wall in their argument, the more determined he became.

"You'll sell the land at the point of a gun, with me holding it on you," she threatened.

Patrick didn't doubt it. Poor, without an inch of land to call their own before his great success in America, Patrick knew big Mike Byrne and Verna were among the hordes of Irish whose lands went to the English and Scots centuries before. But now that she controlled acres as far as the eye could see, Patrick was convinced his wife wouldn't part with a handful of Daitry land.

Verna continued in a shrewish tone. "Ask that high-and-mighty bitch, Madge Brooks, to lend you the money. She hates me guts, and wants the means to laud it over me. She'll be the first to tell the gentry she rescued your sister from me clutches without it costing her a pretty penny."

Hot coals wouldn't have made Patrick admit to Verna or himself how close he had come to asking Madge to fund the London venture, but he couldn't. When she had hinted at the idea, he had grandly waved her offer away. It was more than enough that she volunteered to chaperon Jane to London and launch her in society. Patrick sighed and decided to try a different tack.

"Verna dear you have never made it a secret that you wanted Jane out of the house," he said more reasonably than he liked. "I know you blame her for the difficulties between us. Now here's your chance to be magnanimous and have the house to yourself. Two women in a household is one too many."

Patrick held his breath. He watched his wife's eyes go from suspicion to interest, and a flicker of hope passed through him. The important thing was to make Verna think it was her idea. He motioned her to join him in the enormous leather chair that was his refuge when family and life got too much for him. He had never before invited Verna to share the chair with him.

"What do you say, love?" He waited, not sure the seed had been firmly planted.

"And I thought you never knew how I felt," she said as she burrowed herself beside him. "Put that way, maybe I can prod a bit out of me old da."

"A thousand pounds?" Patrick had only the faintest idea how much it would take to get a girl like Jane properly underway in London, but that much money seemed an enormous sum to him nowadays.

Verna turned in the chair."Are you daft? Know what I could do with that around the estate?"

Patrick knew to a farthing what the sum could do for the place. But his loyalty to Jane took precedence. He had wasted a fortune gallivanting around London in his fancy uniforms on prized horses, unlucky at the gaming tables and the turf, and spending untold sovereigns on how many light skirts. He clenched his fists and waited.

"Five hundred, and not a penny more," Verna said, forcing Patrick to look at her. "I want you to myself that much."

Patrick hugged her. He had won the war.

A few minutes later, Verna stopped at Jane's room and told her Patrick was waiting for her.

"You will have 500 pounds for yourself when you go to London, love," Patrick said before Jane closed the library doors. He ignored the fact that Jane had refused his first offer.

"I am not going. It's too late for me."

"You are scared to death to venture beyond Craig Bay, and all this about being too late is just garbage." Patrick said the first thing to come to mind. Watching Jane pale at the charge, he knew he was right. "You are going. What you do in London is your affair, but you'd be an idiot if you stayed here and withered away. Here's your chance to escape. Take it." He dared not tell her what he and Madge had planned for her. This trip was the only salvation open to her. There were no single and eligible men in Craig Bay or twenty miles about. They all went to Dublin or London to marry well.

Jane was struck dumb by Patrick's charge. Was she a coward? Could she be afraid? Was the devil she knew better than the devil she didn't know?

"When was the last time anyone who knew anything about painting saw your work?" Patrick was asking, pressing her. "Don't you want to know how good you are?"

"Or bad?" Jane countered.

"Or bad," be echoed.

Jane felt giddy. Patrick had touched a nerve.

"Can I take lessons with a miniaturist, Pat?" She held her breath.

"Darling, you can throw the money into the Thames as far as I care, just as long as you have a wonderful time and I can look in my shaving mirror again without hating myself."

Chapter Four

"Good God in heaven, what did I do to deserve this?" Alexander Barrington stormed, throwing the half-read letter across the room to join a growing pile in front of the fire. Later Atkins, his valet-cum-sparring partner, would place them in the corners of the mirror over the fireplace to be considered or discarded. There simply wasn't enough time in the day or night for Alex to attend all the balls, dinner parties, musical evenings, routs, water parties, and picnics on offer. A hostess might pretend to be shocked by his reputation, but that didn't keep her from wanting him to grace her parties.

Alex attacked his breakfast of steak and beer with the same anger he felt at the French at Waterloo, and with the same result. His stomach revolted.

What ever propelled him to read that letter of all those on the silver salver, especially when he was feeling as well as he was likely to feel these days? A long, brisk ride in the park on his new stallion sent over by Tattersall's the day before, a few bruising rounds with Atkins, and a bracing cold bath had given him a ravenous appetite. Daitry's letter took that away soon enough.

Retrieving the letter, he bellowed for Atkins in his best army voice.

"You called, sir?"

"Take this slop away, and bring me the brandy bottle."

"Drinking so early, sir?"

"None of your damned business," Alex said, then, recalling Atkins' years of loyalty, added, "Sorry, I'm blue-deviled again."

Atkins nodded and left to fetch the brandy.

Thinking of Patrick reminded Alex of one of his many grievances against the British Army, politicians, and the generals who ran it. This led him to think about the day he had saved Daitry's life. Wounded by a saber thrust, Patrick's horse had pinned him to the blood-soaked ground. Alex found him writhing and begging for help, and took him back to the surgeon's tent in the rear. Patrick had lost a great quantity of blood, and his right leg was badly mangled. In the ensuing months, the army patched him up and then washed their hands of the Irishman, until Alex took him in hand.

He saw that Patrick received the expert care of Dr. William Lawrence in London, one of the most respected medical men in Europe. When Patrick was finally fit to travel, Alex had taken him back to Ireland. There was no one else to do it. Patrick had no money to travel.

Well-breached himself, Alex never forgot the sacrifices men like Patrick Daitry or the countless lower-class soldiers made for England. In truth, all countries were guilty. They bled their young men in senseless battles and then discarded them until they needed them for another round of slaughter.

Alex thought back to the shock he had felt when he first saw Daitry Hall. A noble house with once-wonderful gardens, the family had certainly fallen on hard times, and Patrick was in no state to bring it back to its former glory. He immediately offered Patrick a loan to make a start on fixing the estate, but Patrick was terrible in his refusal.

"I am already indebted to you, sir, beyond anything I can ever hope to repay," Patrick had said, tears in his eyes as they sat over port on Alexander's last night at

Daitry Hall. "I shall never call upon you again. That's a solemn promise."

The agony it must have meant to ask a favor now was clear in every word of the short letter, making it even more painful for Alexander to ignore. He read the letter through again and gritted his teeth.

"My Lord:
I take pen in hand to break the promise I made to you. I have little alternative. Domestic circumstances, about which I will not trouble you, have led to my sister Jane's journey to London. She will be in the company of a dear friend, Mrs. Margaret Brooks, at the residence of her brother, Lord James Manley, in Hanover Square."

Here Alexander let out an ill-bred snort. Madge Brook was the least of his admirers, and that made the whole affair even more unpleasant. The lady was, in fact, his sworn enemy. She had been the close friend of a family whose efforts to snare him as a son-in-law had ended unpleasantly many years before. Alexander shrugged. Life was one bloody circle. He went on to finish the letter with even less charity.

"My sister, whom you may remember as a quiet person, will not call upon you, and, she must never know of my intrusion upon your kind heart. She is passionately devoted to her drawing and painting, and has no interest in social life.
I ask only that you watch over her from afar. I cannot stress too strongly, my lord, how much my sister will hate it if she ever learns I have asked you this immense favor. She is independent and loyal to a fault. She is a true artist. That is her whole life. I desperately want her to be happy."

Alex threw the letter at the fireplace again, and this time it landed in the path of a tall, broad-shouldered man who entered at the same moment.

"I say, Barrington, don't hit me before I say hello" John Lear laughed and reaching down for the letter, he held it to his nose. "No scent. Are you losing your charm, old man?"

Alex was overjoyed at the unexpected sight of his old school friend. Lear had spent the last four years in America eating his heart out for love of Lady Colby Mannering a towering beauty noted for her sharp tongue and tender heart. She was now the wife of Lord Nevil Browning, a man high in the corridors of power in Whitehall. Lady Colby and Lady Barbara Maitland, a gentle woman of exquisite sense and sensibilities, were Alex's particular friends.

"Are you as rich as they say, John?" Alex asked, coming around the long dining table to embrace his bronzed friend. "'Vicar's son wrests fortune from American savages' Is it true? That's what they say at the clubs, and so says my man of business."

John Lear smiled.

"I found I had a way with a dollar, and with you, Tarn, and Nevil behind me, I did rather well for you and myself. You've seen the results."

Alex listened with half an ear. An idea was germinating in his head, but first he needed some answers.

"Have you seen Lady Colby yet?"

Lear shook his head and blushed.

"If it's still too painful to talk about Colby, please tell me."

"Colby chose the right man. I wasn't Nevil's secretary without knowing the man was a prince. No, I haven't had time to call. I came here directly."

Alex could not have been more pleased. "You'll stay here, of course? The place is a barrack, and you know how welcome you are."

"Actually, I should like it above all else, until I decide what I want to do with the rest of my life," Lear said, grinning. "I'm not sure if I have come back for good or a long visit, and I won't know that until I am here awhile."

And you see Colby, Alex thought, filling in the blank spaces for his friend. Still, nothing could have pleased Alexander Barrington more.

Seeing Lear at his table sharing breakfast and gossip, made Alex realize how lonely he had been. If he missed anything about the army—and he missed everything—it was the daily company of men who shared his memories of the battlefield and the exultation of victory. He longed for his old life dreadfully, no matter how he tried to rebuild his new one. Few diversions helped ease his loss. Gambling for high stakes, Clea, racehorses, and any form of danger could not chase away his gloom.

Suddenly regret swept over Alex, and he put down his brandy glass to stop his hand from shaking and quickly reached for a cheroot. He hoped John didn't see what was happening to him.

One look at Alex after the remove of four years told Lear his friend was in great trouble. Did he regret quitting the army?

"Our friends told me of your departure from the army," Lear said casually. "It was a one-week sensation in the clubs, I'm told. What could have prompted you to throw up everything? You always wanted to be a general by forty."

"Sorry, John. I won't tell you or anyone what happened."

Lear was not surprised. He was sure a great story lay behind Alex's hasty departure from the Guards. Alex's temper was biblical. But while he was often stubborn and rash, Lear had never known Alex to regret any decision he made.

Lear had good reason to understand Alex more than most of their friends. Though poles apart in many ways, Alex had bridged the gap and always had been kind and generous to him. For a simple canon's son, and the grandson of an impoverished baronet, a brilliant scholastic record was not often the road to riches or preferment. With three younger sisters and aging parents, John Lear knew where his future lay. He needed to make money. Without having the nerve to ask any one of his fashionable friends to help him find a good post after university, Alex, on his own, had wangled him the coveted position as secretary to Lord Nevil Browning, and his feet were on the path to the success he now enjoyed.

"Why so thoughtful?" Barrington now asked.

Lear smiled. He was afraid it was not quite the propitious moment to broach Alex about the mess his life had become.

"Not much. Tell me why you were in such a state when I arrived."

Alex pointed to Patrick Daitry's letter and told Lear to read it. Lear scanned the lines quickly.

"I see nothing to put you about," he observed dryly.

"In my experience, dear Lear, women are neither loyal nor independent, and artistic temperament is a facade for bad breath, eccentric clothes, and bad manners. I met enough of them at my mother's knee."

"That's unfair," Lear protested mildly.

"I made the acquaintance of Lady Jane Daitry three years ago. She didn't have a word to say for herself," Alex said. "She was a wraith with dirty fingernails and, though pleasant enough at first, only glowered at me at the end. No, thank you. I will not inflict her on my friends."

"Ah ha." Lear laughed. "One woman in all Christendom who doesn't wet her knickers over you, and you consign her to the dung heap."

"You would say that" Alex grinned.

"I look forward to meeting such a rare creature."

"You shall, my boy, you shall."

Chapter Five

For Jane, the first sight of London made her feel ten feet tall, on the doorstep of heaven.

The six-week journey from Craig Bay to London passed in ever-changing and more brilliant surroundings. Never having been more than ten miles from her home, each day and each mile brought new and fevered sensations. The grand houses and wonderfully kind people she met on Madge Brooks's leisurely procession to England renewed Jane's interest in the world about her for the first time in years.

In her letters to Patrick, she exulted, "I was dead and didn't know it. People I never met before, and probably never will see again, fall over themselves making me welcome and comfortable in their homes. My senses are in turmoil. Grand houses contain art, if not all of the first rank, at least good enough to feast my eyes upon. Aunt Madge has to pull me away from family galleries where portraits of ancestors are a veritable parade of Anglo-Irish history down the ages."

Jane made it a point not to remind her brother of the excellent family portraits, fine miniatures, and good paintings that had been in the Daitry family for years, that had been sold to pay her father's debts. They went the way of the best silver, glass, and anything else her father could lay his hands on in the last years of a spendthrift life. Her bitterness for his wasting Patrick's patrimony had long since faded. But seeing how other people lived in grace and harmony with their heirlooms made her terribly sad. Never would her brother pass on to his children treasures from either side of their family.

Jane was glad to be able to repay in a small way all the wonderful foods and wines lavished on her by offering to make sketches of the families she visited. Everyone seemed delighted, and even Jane, the most difficult critic of all, could be pleased. She rather liked the fuss made over her simple offerings, afraid she would become spoiled with all the attention.

But most of all Jane was grateful for Madge Brooks's company. The older woman was unfailingly good-humored and loving. And, unlike almost everyone else Jane knew, her godmother seemed pleased in her occupation with her charcoals and paints.

"My dear, you are a wonder," Mrs. Brooks said two weeks into their long journey. "You are never bored, idle, or out of sorts, especially when you have your drawing materials at hand."

Jane threw her arms around Madge.

"Do you know, Jane, this is the first time you have ever done that to me?" Madge observed in surprise. "You aren't sickening, are you?"

Jane laughed. It had been so long since she had allowed herself to show her feelings so plainly. This kind and gentle woman, the embodiment of generosity, rapidly chipped away at years of painful reserve behind which the real Jane Daitry hid. She was starved for love and approval, and hadn't realized it until now.

"I am not ill, Aunt Madge. Actually I feel wonderful." How could she have thought that her godmother intended to make an unpaid upper servant of her? Nothing could have been further from the truth. Madge treated her like the daughter she never had, and Jane felt humbled and grateful at the same time.

Now two weeks of living a life of ease in London as

a guest at Lord James Manley's mansion was about to come to an end. Later in the day she and her maid, Lizzie Baines, were going to start another day of hunting for a garret where they could live and paint. London prices were ruinous. The cost of paints, paper, and canvas at Ackermann's repository almost gave her a heart attack. She didn't know how, but she would manage somehow. For more than ever she was determined to be a great miniaturist on the order of Emma Kendrick and Maria Cosway. Nothing less would satisfy her yearning.

But first she needed to paint more heads and study anatomy, and try her hand at portraits to prove she was a serious artist. To do that she needed complete solitude. She didn't want to hurt Aunt Madge and Uncle James, but they were too generous, and wanted to take her out every day. She didn't want to disappoint them, but she did want to paint.

"Jane, you must be seen about the town," Madge urged her every day.

"You must have a smart new wardrobe, and you must allow me to fund one for you. I know more about fashion than you might expect," James told her proudly.

She tried to stand firm, but after much persuasion, she agreed to order a black-and white riding costume. And as if that weren't enough, Uncle James bought her dresses the colors of the rainbow.

"Makes me feel fifty again, buying a young lady satins and lace, He chuckled, enjoying himself.

"You are spoiling me, and I can't permit it, sir," she protested.

"Jane, dear, you must understand that the joy you have brought into my life is worth a hundred riding costumes." He turned to his sister for support.

"Please indulge James. I haven't seen that wicked

gleam in his eyes for years. He reigned supreme in his day, flirting with all the goers."

Now however, time was running out. She had dawdled at dressmakers, milliners, museums, and picture galleries aplenty. Her painting was suffering, and her conscience gave her no rest. It was time to go to work.

Chapter Six

"Don't rush me, Lear," Alex Barrington bellowed loud enough to make passersby stare. "I'll see Jane Daitry when I am good and ready, and not before."

"You said that weeks ago, and if you haven't a conscience, I do. She needs watching over."

For all his protests, Alex was delighted with the way his scheme was falling out. He had laid a gentle trap, and John Lear had fallen into it without a murmur. John's interest in Jane Daitry was well and truly piqued. If he continued to play his cards right, Lear would relieve him of the burden of getting Lady Jane settled nicely. Helping Patrick's sister was preying on his mind far more than he wanted to admit.

From a few discreet inquiries among men of his old regiment, Alex had learned things about the Daitrys that concerned him. Rumor had it that Patrick was married to an unsuitable, jumped-up harridan, and the estate was more rundown than ever. Obviously Patrick's sister was in England on a hunt for a rich husband, however much her brother avoided the subject in his brief letter. Nothing unusual there.

Every season, people of limited means beggared themselves coming to London chasing the dream of a suitable marriage for their offspring, young men as well as green girls. It was for many an embarrassing spectacle. Alex sympathized with young girls who were not raving beauties and men who were not good-

looking or were poor of purse. They were the most un-
likely to take at once. It could only be hell for those
passed over year after year.

Alex shook himself free of the doldrums that had un-
expectedly seized him. No matter how Patrick couched
his letter, his sister would catch cold setting her cap for
case-hardened types like himself.

However John Lear was different. In the weeks since
his return, his friend had made no secret of wanting to
find a wife and set up a nursery. Thank heaven John's
infatuation for Colby was at an end. John's kind heart
and disturbing penchant for difficult women made
him a very convenient candidate for escorting Lady
Jane about, and Alex was doing his best to make Lear
feel it was his duty to aid her.

In the end, Lear and Lady Jane might deal well together, and Mrs. Brooks could not have any objections
to a canon's son who had done well in America. He
might not be a top o' the trees man about town, but he
was eminently suitable and honorable in the extreme.

As for the young lady, she could count herself lucky
to have someone handsome and personable dancing
attendance on her. At that point Alex would feel he
had done his duty by Patrick Daitry and could go on
about his business.

However, Mrs. Brooks, with Lady Jane in tow, were
invisible as far as he could tell. Alex would hate anyone knowing that he had been on the secret prowl for a
glimpse of the ungainly Irish woman ever since he had
received her brother's letter. He had even set foot in
Almack's for the first time in years, nearly paralyzing
Sally Jersey and her coterie of vampires and mothers
chaperoning their hopeful daughters. Of course, he
had beaten a hasty retreat and afterward had repaired
to White's in need of strong drink and male compan-
ionship. Caring about other people was fine in the
army. That was a job he liked. But in civilian life it

could be fatiguing. He couldn't wait to be free of the job Patrick had given him.

"Straighten your cravat and take that sour look off your face," Lear whispered as they came abreast of Manley's town house. "Behave yourself. It's only a morning visit, and we shall be away soon enough."

"Yes. But if Mrs. Brooks has me thrown out on my ear, it will be on your head," Alex growled. "You haven't changed. Still too soft by half. Anyone can steal your heart or your pocketbook."

Lear chuckled and led the way. Looming ahead of them was a gleaming black door. It had rained early that morning, and John scraped the mud off his boots, insisting Alex do the same.

He complied, all at once uncomfortable about facing the formidable Madge Brooks. Perhaps she would refuse to see them, in which case he would leave as fast as his feet would take him, and John could come back alone another day.

Lear had no such qualms, and raised the knocker. The door swung open, leaving both men staring at Lord James Manley's grand, massive-chested butler. The man's greeting was wholehearted, so much so that Barrington had the distinct impression that visitors, particularly young male callers, were very welcome at the house.

The butler took their calling cards and white nosegays and asked them to wait in a side room.

Abovestairs, Lord James Manley read the names, and his florid, cheerful face broke into a grin.

"This is famous, Barrett," Manley said. Crippled by gout and far too stout for his weak heart, Manley was impatient to meet his guests. He took the butler's arm. "Thank God my sister is out. Give me a moment with the gentlemen and then bring Lady Jane to the morning room."

Manley continued to chuckle all the way down the

broad, curving staircase, amused to think how Madge would explode when she learned that Alexander Barrington had come calling on their Jane. His sister had told him about Barrington's connection with Jane's brother. He thought the Earl of Trent would add to Jane's consequence, although he didn't have the nerve to tell this to Madge. She had taken Barrington in dislike because of his many scandals, and wasn't likely to soften toward him.

His fondness for Jane grew with every hour she was under his roof. From what he could see, and from what Madge told him, Jane deserved the best of everything, and he would see she had everything she had missed, if she would only allow him to be generous.

At the bottom of the stairs the old man threw off his servant's arm and walked into the morning room.

"My dear Trent," Manley exclaimed, extending his hand, "I am so seldom in society, but I hear all manner of things about you."

Manley saw Alex stiffen at his words, and was instantly sorry he had said anything. He knew the whole story, one of the few in London who did, and sympathized with all the reasons Alex turned his back on a shining military future. His friend, the Duke of Wellington, had sworn him to secrecy. If only he could tell Alex how much he admired him.

Alex introduced Lear.

"Are you Carlton Lear's son?" Manley asked, studying the handsome newcomer. "I was ahead of him at Oxford, and you are very like the way he looked at eighteen."

Lear nodded and smiled.

"He was a brilliant young fellow, and of course not at all my style. I was a hellion and good for nothing, but I do remember him," Manley recalled. "Give him my best."

In a short time Lear and Manley were joined in admiration of John's father, and the men were talking in a desultory way when the door opened and Jane appeared in the doorway.

Alex was keenly disappointed. Little had changed. Lady Jane appeared unkempt and smeared as ever with paint on her face, her wild, black hair hanging behind her head like a mane. She wore the same nondescript riding clothes as when she prowled her family estate in Ireland. Mrs. Brooks and her brother had their work cut out for them. Jane Daitry was as impossibly shabby as ever, not at all appealing. Jane would never take in London, unless she smartened herself up considerably.

"You!" Jane burst out. The last person in the world she wanted to interrupt her work for stood up, looking sleek and unfeeling as ever. Oh, why hadn't she changed her clothes and combed her hair? The butler had asked if she wanted to change her clothes, but she was so disturbed by the interruption she hadn't taken the hint. If he had said there were guests, she hadn't heard it.

"Jane, really," Manley protested.

He hastily made the introductions.

Alex was amused. It wasn't often young women responded to him in such a way, although, according to his mother, he might profit by the experience. Now that he thought about it, he had not been the nicest houseguest when he had stayed at Craig Bay either.

Thinking about it now, Alex could imagine he must have appeared boorish and thick. The worst sin must have been the last night, when he edged Jane off the piano bench. She was a good musician, he remembered that, but her phrasing was off, and he couldn't resist showing her how the Mozart sonata should be played.

He hadn't meant to offend her. Was she one of those women who remembered every hurt? Well, London would cure her of delicate sensibilities in no time at all.

She would have to learn to protect her tender feelings, and no one could help her there.

Manley, John, and Jane were now talking animatedly, ignoring him, he was delighted to see, when the door behind him opened and closed with a decided click of disapproval. It might have been described as an angry slam, but the sound was welcome anyway. Alex was anxious to bring the visit to a close as quickly as possible. Lady Jane was making him uncomfortable, and he wasn't used to being made to feel a fifth wheel.

"Really, James, this is not well done," Madge Brooks called out harshly, obviously not in the least pleased with the tableau she found before her. "An unmarried girl entertaining three gentlemen without a chaperon is most irregular."

James Manley rose slowly to his feet.

"How right you are, my dear, but you must know how careless I am about such things," he said easily. "It was entirely my fault, but unless my eyes mistake me, my housekeeper is just beyond the far door protecting our reputations."

Lord James introduced his sister to John Lear. He knew she didn't approve of the Earl of Trent and so passed over the name hurriedly. His sister harrumphed and was silent, and the visit concluded shortly thereafter on a grim note.

They left as quickly as good manners dictated.

"Tell me, what did you think of Lady Jane?" Alex asked as soon as the door closed on them.

"I found her charming, unspoiled, so out of the common way," Lear enthused.

Alex was delighted. His plan might work. John was evidently interested, though how any man could be smitten with Jane Daitry was beyond him. She reminded him of a high-spirited black horse gamboling in an Irish pasture. He liked his women sleek and feline, Clea Wesley to a T. Women like Jane Daitry bored him to tears, made him nervous actually, as if they weighed him and found him wanting. She was too much like the female writers and poets who cluttered his mother's drawing room, battening on her generosity and soft heart.

"Are you about to adopt another waif and stray?" Alex asked, leading a fast pace away from Hanover Square. "Judging by past performance, a woman can be any size or form, as long as she has problems and you can play the gallant to the hilt." He was thinking of Colby Browning née Colby Mannering, for one, once poorer than a church mouse, with the tartest tongue in all Christendom. "Colby, at least, was beautiful and came from a good English family, however improvident."

John Lear turned an angry face on Alex.

"Sometimes, Barrington, I think you are turning into a cad, and other times I know it."

Alex reared back, his hands white-knuckled fists, ready to pummel Lear. Then he dropped his hands and turned away.

"You presume too much."

"I am mortally ashamed of you, James," Madge Brooks proclaimed. "Alexander Barrington in this house. How could you?"

Manley was properly repentant, but soon his patience gave out.

"My dear girl, do stop. No harm was done," Manley said when he could get a word in. "Jane won't allow us to take her where she can meet eligible men, and I don't see a flood of 'em on our doorstep. I, for one, will not have her languishing without lifting a finger to give her a chance to have a husband and a family of her own."

Indeed, Madge knew that her brother, a practiced ladies' man, who had neither a wife nor children, never wanting anything of a permanent arrangement, had taken to Jane the moment they arrived. Jane basked in his approval so charmingly that Madge felt her heart brim over with happiness. It was years since she had seen both Manley so happy and jolly and Jane so perfectly at ease with herself.

And, of course, James was right, Madge conceded. Jane, with her fear of being a burden, went to maddening extremes. If they permitted her, she would have become an unpaid servant, insisting on waiting on them. The girl was anything but a burden. Her good nature and happy disposition, never given proper reign at Daitry Hall had blossomed wonderfully in the months since they had left Ireland.

"Perhaps you're right, but I'm still cross with you, James," Madge continued. "Why did you permit Jane to meet the gentlemen in that regalia of hers? I don't give a fig about Barrington, but I do like Mr. Lear. He's a gentleman. I hope he was not put off by Jane's appearance."

"And what are you cooking up in that head of yours, Madge?" her brother interrupted. He knew his sister well. Only something pleasant could deflect her annoyance toward him.

"I think you may be right," she said with a satisfied smile. "I shall detach nice Mr. Lear from that terrible Lord Alexander and see that he plays escort for Jane."

"You mean a Judas goat leading men to our door" Manley chuckled.

"No." She grinned. "I think he'd make a perfect husband for our Jane."

"With a little managing by you?"

"Of course!"

Chapter Seven

After a fast-paced ride in Hyde Park, Alex came into Portman Square, not in the least pleased to see Clea Wesley's carriage waiting at his doorstep.

What the hell was she doing paying him a morning call? He was furious, but then again, he wasn't pleased with many things, and hadn't been for weeks.

His quarrel with Lear had upset him terribly. He was trying to steel himself to apologize, and until John forgave him wholeheartedly, he could not be comfortable with himself.

Was John right? Was he a cad? He knew better than anyone that he flouted society's more restrictive conventions. He was often careless, certainly short tempered, impatient, not always as polite or charming as he should be. His manners might be wanting, but in his private code of conduct hurting anyone, cruelty, cheating, or stealing were not permissible. Hadn't he proven his love of God, King, and Country, risked and lost the very thing that meant so much to him? He had very nearly lost his sanity telling his superiors that Colonel Ralph Brinton, a decorated hero, was a spy for Napoleon and had been for years.

Despite his reputation to the contrary, he never forced a woman to submit to him, or consciously treated one shabbily. Alex smiled ruefully. However no one would ever convince Madge Brooks of his honor toward women. She was the perfect example of someone who thought she knew the real Alexander

Barrington. The memory of the way she had treated him like a noxious snake under her foot still nettled far more than he wanted to admit.

He knew what troubled Madge Brooks most. She believed, like so many others, that he had jilted Pamela Britton-Steen, when in fact nothing was further from the truth. The young lady had found herself pregnant and when the man refused to marry her, she had tried to inveigle Alex. He had almost married her out of pity, but she miscarried, and he never again allowed his heart to compromise his brain.

As for Clea Wesley, she neither pretended nor wanted anything more than excitement in bed. Once she had told him she lived her life as a man, taking her pleasures where and when she found them, and the hell with the consequences. It shocked him, but he had accepted it. They kept each other amused and satisfied, and until recently it had been enough for the two of them. If she ever wanted more, and he saw no signs she did, that was a possibility he would have to deal with when the time came. Thank heaven she had given up arranging a marriage for him.

Alex shuddered. What was the matter with him, dredging up old scandals and new worries? Between Mrs. Brooks's open dislike, Jane Daitry's disdain, and John Lear's charge against his character, he was feeling raw and battered.

Was it time he changed his ways? Perhaps.

Alex felt better and rode quickly to his house to confront Clea. He could see that his butler and Atkins were as displeased with Clea's behavior as he was. Married or unmarried ladies did not visit a bachelor's residence early in the morning.

He followed his butler to the music room.

"Darling, at long last," Clea threw herself at him, her abigail all but fading into the yellow window coverings across the room.

"Jenner, you may wait outside the door," Clea ordered.

Alex countermanded, "Miss Jenner, please leave the door open. Lady Clea is leaving soon."

Furious, Clea turned on him.

"You have not been near me in ages," she cried. Then she saw Alex's jaw tighten, and realized she had made a terrible mistake coming to his house. It was a measure of her desperation that she couldn't stop herself. Her body ached for him and overrode her good sense. She had to see him at whatever price.

Alex picked up Clea's violet pelisse with the magnificent diamond pin he had commissioned Tessier of Bond Street to make for her. It had set him back a pretty penny, but he knew she liked him buying her presents and he had wanted to make her happy.

"Now, dear girl, I think it is time you left."

"I could throttle my husband and my daughter," Clea said, pulling her wrap out of his hands and throwing it over a sofa. "Their damn ambitions have driven you away. My offering you Mabel was a bad mistake; wasn't it?"

"Don't be silly, Clea dear," Alex said, going in search of the pelisse. "You owe your family your first loyalty, and we both agreed we have been a bit too open in our behavior. Haven't we?"

Clea's eyes blazed. He was tired of her, and she had handed him a perfect excuse to end their affair. Suddenly she felt old and bitter and wanted to strike out at him. She turned away to gain time to collect herself. She was a fighter, and the Earl of Trent was worth fighting for. She would not give him up without a struggle, but she wouldn't rush her fences. She was going away in a few days and would plan her campaign carefully.

"Of course, you're right, my darling," Clea said

quickly, letting Alex drape the wrap around her shoulders.

Alex was relieved at the ease with which he had propelled Clea out of his house. He knew her temper, and he was in no mood to engage in a dustup.

He saw her off and walked back to his book room, determined to track down John Lear and make his apologies. Lear had moved out of Alex's house and into his club the afternoon of their quarrel. He missed the man's company sorely. Perhaps other vicars' sons needed to kick over the traces, but John Lear was probity itself, upright, moral, and expecting the same from all around him.

Alex had no idea how John was occupying himself. He had been scouring the clubs and the hotels, but he hadn't seen a sign of him, and the few people he had asked were not helpful at all.

He dashed off a note to Lear at his club asking for a meeting, sealed it with the intaglio ring on his small finger, and ordered his butler to see that it was delivered.

Feeling better, he rose from his writing desk and went upstairs in search of Atkins. He had a dinner meeting with a few of his wealthiest friends to plan a strategy for helping servicemen. He was looking forward to a long and productive evening. Perhaps in the end he could assuage his badly bruised ego and do some good for the men who had served under him and others who had fought in the wars with Napoleon. He fervently hoped so.

Chapter Eight

The small tea party drew to a close, but still John Lear and Aunt Madge talked and gossiped about people and London goings-on, a topic that had long since palled on Jane and James Manley.

Jane hoped her impatience didn't show, but she had too much on her plate. She wanted to tell her host and hostess her good news and then return to the studio before nightfall. For all that the attics she now used at the top of the house were depressing, they were luxurious compared to the garret she had rented earlier today. Tomorrow she and Lizzie would return with buckets, lye, and whitewash to try to make the place habitable.

Jane had seen far better and more costly accommodations, but she couldn't afford to be too particular in her preferences. The serious inroads she had made into the money Patrick had given her were alarming. She needed furniture, bed clothing, dishes, and heaven knew what else. Domesticity had never been her strong suit, and here she was planning to set up house and studio with no one to guide her and no money to spare. But she and Lizzie would manage. They had to.

She desperately needed a comprehensive portfolio of her best work to show a teacher of miniatures, who would take her on as a pupil. With luck, he might be someone kind who remembered his own early struggles and would be tolerant of her small gifts. She dared not dream she would be taken on by anyone as famous as Emma Kendrick. She was too much the novice, and even in her wildest dreams knew she wasn't a natural miniaturist. But that wouldn't stop her. She never wavered in her desires.

Her ambitions and determination would overcome every obstacle. Failure wasn't possible. In the next few weeks she would begin her search. From her earliest memories, she had been in love with miniatures, and she would never deviate from the path she had chosen. She knew she was a fair portraitist, and had a unique presentation. Why couldn't she be content with what she was already good at? She had no answer to that, and it made her shift uncomfortably in her seat. She caught Uncle James yawning behind his hand. They smiled at each other, easy conspirators.

"Jane, do something," Manley whispered to her.

"I couldn't" she giggled.

He winked at her then said aloud, "I say, Madge, I think it's time I showed all of you a surprise I have been preparing."

"Before you do that, sir, I should like to tell you something," Jane interposed. She meant to spring her news without an audience, but it seemed that John Lear would never depart. He had called on them every day, and while pleased to see him, he was affecting her progress. His visits delighted Madge, and several times he stayed to dinner. Jane liked him well enough, but his presence in the house meant she had to abandon her work and make herself presentable, for Madge had seen to it that there would not be a repetition of the way she had looked the first time Lear had called on them. These interruptions to visit with him sorely tried her patience and made removing herself from Lord James's home a pressing necessity.

At last she couldn't control her impatience.

"I have found a studio. Lizzie and I move in tomorrow," she blurted out.

Lord James and his sister stared at her in disappointment. She could have bitten her tongue for not choosing the right moment and the right words to tell them of her decision.

"You've spoiled my surprise," Manley said sadly, rising painfully. "Still, come and see what I have prepared for you, my dear, and then make up your mind."

He led the others toward the French doors at the back of the house. There, at the bottom of a large garden loomed a greenhouse, where six men cleaned glass panes and others planted shrubs at the base.

Forgetting his first disappointment, Manley's eyes filled as he watched Jane. It was obvious she was overcome. The greenhouse had been turned into a lavish artist's studio with every refinement she could desire.

"I don't believe it," Jane cried, unable to accept that the studio was meant for her. Inside, she ran her hands over the first professional easel she had ever seen. Stacks of canvases peeked out from narrow slots made especially for them, and an army of paints arrayed like the rainbow made her itch to touch them. There were candleholders and candles enough to light up the dreariest night, and dominating everything, was a dais on which sat a classic Greek couch draped in the richest materials.

Jane didn't know where to look next. Tears of joy filled her eyes, and her feet were rooted to the heavy green carpet covering an irregular brick floor.

"Please don't refuse me," James Manley whispered. He wanted to give Jane the moon and see her always as she looked now, eyes blazing joy, face flushed with wonder. He would do anything to keep her near. He cursed the blindness of youth, when he had chosen the pleasures of the flesh and the table over a wife and children. He thought of Jane as the daughter any man would want, young, fearless, arms open wide for life and the coming dawn.

Jane wiped away her tears.

"I don't deserve all this," she kept murmuring when she found her breath.

Afraid of intruding, Madge signaled John Lear to follow her, and together they quit the studio.

"I cannot imagine anything to please Lady Jane more," Lear said, assisting his hostess back to the house. "I hope your brother's generosity cures the good lady's restlessness."

Madge didn't think her brother's surprise would do anything of the sort. She was completely out of charity with James. With a studio so perfect, Jane would never give a moment's thought to marriage.

She was very nearly losing patience with Lear, too, especially since she had high hopes for an announcement of a betrothal. Mooning over Jane's every move and every utterance might turn the heads and raise the expectations in the breasts of most susceptible young women, but not Jane Daitry.

Madge wasn't sure who infuriated her more, James for not consulting her about the studio, or John Lear, who was so nice, but so dull. He was clearly at a standstill, and didn't know what to do to secure Jane's interest. Men! Why couldn't they leave things to women with their wiser heads and good commonsense?

As for Jane, she was fast despairing there as well. Madge was sure they would all see less and less of her. She didn't know whether to cry or stamp her feet.

Madge bade goodbye to Lear, barely able to contain her temper, and went up to her room to rest before dinner.

John Lear departed Manley House a little depressed. He knew Jane Daitry liked him well enough, but she never gave him a particle of encouragement. He wasn't in love with her, but that would come in the weeks ahead. He had no doubt at all. Not since his hopeless infatuation with Colby Browning had he felt so taken with another woman.

Jane might not be as flamboyant as Colby, but the two shared depths of feeling and a single-mindedness he found enormously attractive and a little daunting at times. They were women who, once committed to an ideal, would never let anything interfere. Colby had been determined to see her family safe, and Jane wanted to be the very best painter she could be. He admired determination, for it was what had made him a rich man against tremendous odds.

Lear knew he wasn't the most colorful of men, but he prided himself on being an honest one, and in the right moment he would put his heart at Jane's feet with the certainty she would accept him. He expected Jane's ambitions to become more moderate with a husband and home of her own and children to distract her. It seemed to have done so for Colby, who was now a subdued matron. His love would be all in all to Jane. He wasn't going to think beyond that certainty. Proceeding with a jaunty step, he started for his club. A few blocks further on he recalled he was close to Alex's house. He stopped, lit a cheroot, and went on at a slower pace. He was sick at heart about Alex. How dare he call his best friend a cad? If it weren't for Alex's kindnesses to him, the money he had pressed on him years before, he could never have gone to America and begun the business that was the start of his good fortune. How dare he question Alex? He owed him an apology, and would not delay delivering it.

Chapter Nine

Alexander Barrington hovered over his leather and brass-top desk, covered in an inch-thick layer of papers, maps, and architectural plans dealing with the Legion, the name he had chosen for his organization.

A gentle knock on the door recalled him from the list of names and broadsheets he was studying. He waited for the butler to enter.

"My lord, Mr. Lear wishes to see you," the butler announced.

Alex threw down his pen and came around the desk to await Lear at the door. How good of John to respond so quickly to his note.

"I would gladly have come to you," he said hoarsely, not trusting his voice. "So like you to make matters easy for me, John."

Lear looked confused.

"I sent you a note," Alex explained. "Been looking for you everywhere."

"I am abjectly sorry that I said such a cruel thing to you," Lear hastened to say. "After all you have done for me, how ungrateful I must seem"

Alex clapped him on the back and rang for a servant. His butler arrived at once.

"Bring up the best champagne," he said, turning to Lear once again. "Thank you for reminding me that I have become impossible."

"Alex, don't embarrass me. I had no right to insult you. I do prefer you when you swagger."

"You know me well." Alex laughed. "Now, tell me where have you been?" Alex requested cheerfully, showing the way to massive red leather chairs flanking a roaring fire. It was spring, but cool with a hint of storm in the air. "I've scoured the town for you."

"Actually, I have been seeing something of Lady Jane Daitry," he said, trying to appear offhand.

Alex was delighted. His scheme to bring them together had succeeded far sooner than he had hoped.

"Mrs. Brooks should be delighted," Alex said, feeling better than he had in days. "Where has that ogress permitted you to escort the young lady?"

"Nowhere to speak of, but that's not all Mrs. Brook's fault. Lady Jane is not fond of society and would rather be closeted in her studio. You should see what Manley has done to an old greenhouse," Lear said, smiling.

"Have you seen any of her work?" Alex asked idly.

"She is very secretive about her paintings. Mrs. Brooks said she's only seen some sketches, and they were very nice. You know women, they must have bits of drama in their lives."

Somehow Alex wasn't convinced that Jane Daitry was merely harboring a charming pastime. His visit to Ireland and, later, the morning visit at the Manleys' suggested something else, but what exactly it was escaped him. Women of his acquaintance, whatever age, would never appear before a gentleman without every hair in place and wearing the handsomest gown in her wardrobe.

Every time he had seen Jane Daitry, her face had been streaked, her hands caked, nails broken, and her clothes old and in the very worst taste. Odd indeed. He never imagined Madge Brooks would be willing to tolerate a badly dressed woman living under her protection. Then he thought of the words in Patrick's letter. "She is independent to a fault and devoted to her art."

At once, Alex was far more interested in Jane Daitry than he had expected to be. She had the merit, at least, of being an original, and in conventional, hide-bound London a young woman of real spirit, and artistic as well, might be fun to watch.

Chapter Ten

"This is sheer heaven, and I can't thank you enough," Jane said sleepily. "You make me feel blessed and humble."

It was past midnight and she was talking to James Manley, the first guest she had permitted into the studio. They were sitting over the last of the tea in the heavy crockery she used when she worked.

"Aren't you cold?" he asked, pulling the collar of his splendid Gieves and Hawkes brocaded dressing gown closer. "I must tell Barrett you need a larger fireplace. This place is like a tomb."

"No, it isn't," she protested. "It's perfect. I can't imagine Reynolds or Lawrence occupied a studio half as splendid as this."

"Does it help your work?"

"How can you ask? Look at all I've done in five weeks. The work flows out of me like a spring."

Manley smiled to himself. He knew as well as Jane how hard she worked and the long hours she spent in the greenhouse when the household thought she was sleeping. He spent long periods of time secretly watching over her. They were the most satisfying moments of his days. Before she came into his life, Manley wondered how he would get through each day. Now there weren't enough hours. He was her guardian angel, and he meant to continue until the end of his life.

"I can see you are productive, but are you pleased with what you're doing?"

"I am never completely pleased, but that doesn't worry me as it once did," Jane said happily, returning to the dais where he sat.

"Good. Now I'll let you go back to work," he said, rising from the chair. He had seen what he wanted to see. Jane was happy. The watchman he had secretly hired to keep her safe was awake and sitting quietly out of sight. There wasn't anything she lacked. "Get some rest, my dear. Madge is beside herself. The Bellinghams' party is the biggest event of the season. Madge is planning it as your unofficial come-out, and is nervous as a cat. Do her proud, won't you?"

Jane walked him to the door and kissed him on the cheek. Then she handed him a branch of candles and looked out into the night. "May I walk you to your room?"

"No, thank you, my dear. Barrett is waiting for me."

Jane waved him off and went back to work. She uncovered the study she was making of Manley's head. It was to be a surprise for his birthday in a few months.

As usual, Jane was frightened of falling short and making a miserable mull of their expectations. Had she captured James's goodness, his wisdom? He was the kindest man she had ever met, but could she make everyone understand what she wanted them to see? Patrick It was a fear she always faced when she began each painting. The enormity of it made her giddy. She stretched the muscles of her neck and closed her eyes, trying to ease the tiredness. Nothing helped, and she decided to go to bed to be fresh for tomorrow.

Jane finished dressing for the Bellingham party.

"Patrick would be so proud, my dear, Jane," Madge said, stemming tears with a small handkerchief. "I once thought your mother was the most regal woman I ever knew. She couldn't hold a candle to you tonight."

"If I were forty years younger," James Manley said, finishing a thorough examination of Jane, "I'd send John Lear to China, and you and I would fly to Gretna Green."

"Uncle James, please. Mr. Lear and I . . ."

"Only just met? Ha. He's a slow coach. Needs some steel in his wheels" Manley brought his hand from behind his back. He extricated a black velvet box, opened it, and held out a magnificent tiara.

"Perfect diamonds," Madge said, examining the piece like a trader.

"Just like a rainbow, my jewelry chap assured me, and made for the perfect woman. Madge has enough jewelry, and so I thought of you. Fitting. Not another word. Give me the pleasure of putting this on your head."

Jane backed away.

"I can't wear it."

"Won't take it back. I got it from under the nose of Prinny," Manley chuckled. "Not the first time I did that, I'll have you know."

"I can't. I'd feel an impostor. I've done nothing to deserve such luxury."

"Only brought sunshine to this house," Madge said. "Now stop all this nonsense and bend your head."

"I'll wear it tonight, but I won't keep it," Jane said after Madge propelled her toward a mirror and made her look at herself.

"You aren't natural, my girl. Anyone else would be ecstatic," Madge muttered.

At that, John Lear walked into the drawing room behind the butler.

"Lady Jane, you look ravishing," he said, his eyes riveted.

Jane looked at her friends and their admiring faces. Is this the way women feel when they are cherished and admired? What an experience! It had never been her lot to be loved and thought of as someone special. All her life she had been plain Jane Daitry.

She was Cinderella, for one night at least, and she would enjoy the role to the fullest.

Chapter Eleven

"Are you having a nice season?" Alex managed to ask between clenched teeth.

"Lovely, my lord," the girl replied breathlessly. "And you?"

Alex nodded, showing his even white teeth, while he planned an early death, preferably in boiling oil, for Clea Wesley.

"I see you are here with your mother, my lord. Is she well?"

"Very well. And your mother?"

This is what happened when he tried to be a good son. Between his mother asking him to escort her to the Bellinghams' ball and Clea's machinations, he was in a murderous state. He smiled down at his partner. It wasn't her fault Clea had pushed her into his arms and had ordered them to dance.

Only a cad, there was that word again, would leave the poor girl stranded. And so he bowed and swung Mabel Seymour into the stream of couples dancing about the floor as if he desired nothing more than a few precious moments of her company.

Alex smiled down at Mabel, while inside he longed for the interminable music to stop. Marriage. Never. He thought Clea, of all people, knew his mind on the subject. To make matters worse, Clea knew he hated to dance. But it wasn't the poor girl's fault, and he felt sorry for her. Clea, under her silks and flounces, was a battering ram when set on her own course. He often thought Wellington had lost a great field commander when she was born a female.

Mabel Seymour was an innocent, and deserved better. He had seen too much, felt too much to be comfortable with such a simple innocent. And he would be damned if he would allow Mabel to be sacrificed to countenance their affair or for some other nefarious reason of Clea's.

"Have you been on the water much this year, Miss Seymour?" Alex asked, at once attentive and smiling warmly. "The Mayers' gave a splendid party on their yacht, didn't they?"

"I had a dreadful cold, and Mama wouldn't allow me to leave my bed. So unfair."

Alex agreed, and looked around the wall of chaperons and dowagers hoping to see Mabel's mother. Mrs. Seymour was smiling and talking to his mother with great familiarity and animation. He could see his mother wore her most patient smile.

Alex missed a step. The devil. Involving the mothers as well? What might have started as an amusing bit of fun in Clea's clever head had gone beyond the permissible. This was ridiculous.

As he turned back to his companion, Alex's eye caught sight of a woman entering the ballroom wearing a daring dark blue silk dress cut low over a charming bosom. There was a blinding tiara in midnight black hair and she was smiling in a most beguiling manner.

Alex almost collided with another couple, his eyes scanning over Mabel's head for a closer look at the newcomer.

The woman had presence and animation, and her smile was dazzling. It drew him like a magnet. Only the presence of Madge Brooks on one side of her and John Lear on the other told him Jane Daitry had arrived.

The wonders that a good modiste and a flattering coiffure could do for a woman were hardly unknown to Alex. He had paid enough for such services in his time to have a thoroughgoing knowledge of their considerable skills.

But he couldn't believe he had been so blind. Jane Daitry might not be a Clea Wesley, the kind of petite, curvy, high-bosomed woman he preferred, but now, taking another look at her, Lady Jane had little reason to hang back. With her regal air, extraordinary eyes, height, and luminescent skin, he no longer felt he had done an injustice to his friend John Lear by pushing him into Jane's arms. Lear's interest in her must be a magical elixir for the usually remote, awkward girl, Alex concluded. There was nothing better for looks and complexion than the attentions of a handsome man.

Alex was ashamed of himself. It had been his own stupid blindness. Jane was Patrick's young sister, and he had not looked further than her disheveled appearance and what he now suspected must be a terrible shyness. Lucky John, clearly a connoisseur of women. The years in America must have taught him a thing or two about women.

Across the room, Jane was taken aback to see Alex at the ball dancing with a short, plump young woman so clearly enraptured with him that even from this distance her face lit up like a beacon.

"Is that really Alexander Barrington I see?" Madge hissed in her ear. "I suppose we have been lucky not encountering him before this."

Jane went numb at her first sight of Alex in weeks. He set her nerves dancing much as he cavorted most capriciously in her dreams. Perversely, she was angry with him for not showing the least interest in how she was faring so far from home. On the few occasions she had given in to Aunt Madge's entreaties and Lear's insistence to join them at entertainments, Jane had gone, but only in the secret hope of catching sight of Alex. And now, on the one night she hadn't thought about him, here he was with a young girl in his arms unquestionably thrilling to his practiced addresses.

"Look at Barrington dancing attendance on Sybil Seymour and that daughter of hers." Aunt Madge continued to fill Jane's ears with her dislike of Alex. "Maybe he has found someone to love, but what are her parents thinking? The gel is as nice as she is rich, but I would have thought she was a bit tame for him. You never know with men, but I suppose it's different when one means to set up a nursery. It doesn't hurt when a huge dowry comes with the lady, does it?"

Why should Jane care who he loved? He had never seen her as anything but Patrick's troublesome sister without a penny to her name, with a difficult disposition as well that seemed to bore him. He had been sullen and impatient in Ireland, and a marble statue at Uncle James's house. Enough. She had come to the ball to please Madge. Now she wished to please herself.

"Would you like to dance, Lady Jane," John Lear asked hopefully.

She nodded and took his arm. They joined the others and danced in silence. She couldn't think of a thing to say and tried to look as if she were enjoying herself.

Alex watched them from behind a column, looking for signs of affection between Jane and Lear. Clearly they were enjoying themselves. And why not? He was often weary of hearing John talk about Jane as someone unique and intriguing. He wasn't quite certain John was exaggerating after all.

As the dancers waited for the orchestra to resume Alex abruptly left the sidelines and received Lear's permission to dance with Jane. Alex wasn't sure, but he thought Jane's fingers tightened for a moment at his touch. She was a far more skilled dancer than he, and like a feather on her feet.

"You dance very well, Lady Jane."

"Ireland is not as backward as you English like to think."

"You look very nice tonight," he said, taking command and leading her to the middle of the dance floor. "Are you happy?"

"Yes." Jane's eyes glinted.

"Are you game for a bit of fun?" he teased her. "Shall we bring a bit of life to the place?"

Jane pulled back and saw the mischievous challenge in his pale eyes. She hesitated.

Alex waited, peering at her closely. Madge would have a spasm. And Jane? What was she really made of?

She shrugged her shoulders and smiled shyly at him under her dark lashes. He took it for assent, lifting her off her feet, and it seemed they flew through the air. She had never known such exhilaration, and it pleased her beyond anything. The other couples formed two lines down the ballroom, while they whirled between them.

"Now, my lady, you are launched into society, and I hope you like it." Alex returned her to the sidelines, bowed to a fuming Madge Brooks, winked at a smiling John Lear, and marched out of the room toward the stairs without a backward glance.

"What the hell was that all about?" Clea asked, barring his way, her green eyes on fire, her mouth grim. "Who's that nobody, and why did you single her out for your wild attentions?"

He turned to a furious Clea.

"Why do I do anything?" he asked negligently, taking her hand. "Why did you push poor Mabel on me?"

Clea disregarded his questions.

"Will I be seeing you later?" she asked hopefully.

He nodded and ran down the steps. The last thing he wanted was an assignation, but he owed Clea some loyalty. Feelings of displeasure he didn't understand were warring inside his head. He needed a few hours at his club before he came back to claim his mother.

Jane was not at all happy with herself or Alex. His complete abandonment left her feeling discarded and stupidly at a loss. The minutes in his arms, the most thrilling and exciting she had ever known, were now ashes on her soul.

Alexander Barrington was not a true gentleman. She had said it often, and she said it again. She resolved to cut him out of her life as she would anything else so threatening to her future.

"The man is a fiend, making a fool of you," Madge was saying, looking at Lear as well. "You should have known better and given him a setdown he wouldn't forget."

Jane and John exchanged silent glances. She hadn't the courage to admit how much she had enjoyed every bit of the display. She didn't give a fig about her best interests.

Yet, fearful, she saw a terrible trap ahead. Alexander Barrington was the only person who had ever rivaled her feelings for her work, and admitting that at long last made Jane understand how much she needed to fight against his unwelcome intrusion in her life. She once read, and believed with all her heart, that true artists had only one love, one child, and one home: work. The true artist could not be like other people. Two passions in an artist's life were not permissible. Art was going to be her lover, children, home, and her ultimate comfort. She must accept that, or her life would be a fragmented hell.

Having decided that once and for all time, Jane felt her headache lift, her spirits soar. She was eager to leave, for she longed to be in her studio. It was the only life she wanted. She took John Lear's arm, and the two followed Aunt Madge out of the ballroom to their carriage.

Chapter Twelve

Lord James Manley put down his knife and fork and sipped his tea, waiting for his sister to finish her tirade.

"You are getting hysterical about Alexander Barrington, and I won't hear another word against him."

"How can you defend that man?" Madge asked. "You are just like John Lear. Instead of being outraged, as one might expect, he laughed about it. He said Alex liked to give the ton something to talk about."

"Good for Lear."

"James, Barrington has ruined the girl socially. And if you are half as concerned with her reputation as you profess, you'd . . ."

"Call him out?" Manley laughed.

"Sometimes I think dueling has a way of reminding people just how far they should go before they have to pay for their indiscretions."

"He didn't accost the girl in the middle of the damned party, did he?"

"James, really, such language."

"Madge, all Alex was probably trying to do was to show the other bucks that Jane is alive and worthy of their attention, and, frankly, I think that's a very good thing. I wish I had seen to your welfare when you were young, and then you wouldn't have married that milk-sop, Brooks."

Madge appeared on the verge of apoplexy.

"I am sorry, my dear, your husband was a nice man,

but he was a bit wet. Now be honest and confess. Wasn't he?"

To his surprise and delight, his sister didn't bite off his head.

"He wasn't like you and your riotous friends, if that's what you mean," she said archly.

Emboldened by what he thought was a gleam in her eyes, he went on. "Mark my words. Barrington did our darling Jane a great favor. Watch the flowers delivered to the door this morning."

He hoped the good Lord would forgive him for pretending to second sight. He knew several bouquets were already on their way. His butler had shared a pint at a local tavern early that morning with the local flower seller.

"I always sent pink flowers myself, when I wanted a lady to know that I had warm feelings for her and desired to know her better" Manley sighed, remembering all the yellow flowers he had also sent when he was tiring of a lady and wanted a graceful exit without tears and tirades.

"I hate it when you men stick together," Madge said, breaking into her brother's memories. "I thought Lear had better sense. He said exactly what you said, James. Alexander Barrington acts on impulse and never means harm, but I know better . . . He disgraced Pamela Britton-Steen and did something terrible that caused him to be drummed out of the army."

Manley threw down his napkin.

"You don't know a blasted thing about him," her brother replied, his patience frayed. "Pamela was no better than she should have been, and Alex was a genuine hero. The army was wrong."

Madge was openmouthed. "Really, James."

"And I'll tell you something else. I'd rather see Jane marry a reformed rake than a bumpkin any time of the day."

"I do believe you are drunk or addlepated," Madge snapped at him.

"I am neither, and you know it. All I know is that when a rake decides to turn over a new leaf and marry, he is apt to be a loyal husband and father. He has seen the world and knows how to make a woman happy," James Manley thundered. "And if you take my advice, which you won't, leave the poor girl alone. All Jane cares about is her work. I am sure marriage is the last thing on her mind, unfortunately."

In that, Manley was a bit off the mark.

While they argued, Jane was in her studio beginning a square miniature of Barrington to add to the hidden stores in her bedroom. She had gone to her studio when she returned from the party the night before and, unable to sleep, had lit the candles and begun the piece of work she was now fully engaged in.

She cursed her limited knowledge of the special skills needed to render the likeness she yearned for. Much as she wanted to do a large-scale portrait of Alex, she feared to try, because of Aunt Madge's dislike of the man. But more than that, Jane would have been mortified if anyone suspected her secret *tendre* for Alex Barrington. Although neither Madge nor James came to the studio often, Jane wasn't going to take the chance they would see her preliminary efforts and begin to wonder what she was about.

Jane stopped, pushing aside the sketch. Why did Alexander Barrington capture her imagination long before she ever saw him? A year of letters from Patrick praising his commanding officer for his military exploits and care of the men under his command had fired Jane's imagination. From long years of virtual isolation, she acknowledged grudgingly, she knew less than nothing about men and love, except that it seemed to hurt everyone concerned. It started with her mother's hopeless infatuation with her father, and had ended with Verna's possessive love for Patrick. What could she have seen in the limited life she led at Daitry Hall?

Now the realization that she had arrived at her twenty-sixth year virgin in heart and body, and likely to remain so, seemed a terribly dismal fate. Why had it never seemed so important before?

Voices behind her threw her into further confusion.

"My dear Lady Jane, what is the matter?" John Lear asked worriedly as he entered the studio with Madge Brooks at his side.

Jane had no idea what she must have looked like to bring on their concern, much less this intrusion, and covered the drawing under a pile of other papers on her drawing table. Fortunately, they were just inside the door and could not see what she was doing.

"What lovely flowers, Mr. Lear," she said, hoping her voice masked her very real annoyance at the interruption. "You are abroad early this morning."

"Mr. Lear has decided to go into the country to visit his family, my dear," Madge explained brightly. "He's come to say good-bye."

"I have sadly neglected my parents," John said. "Furthermore I am hoping to buy a gentleman's residence. I have decided to sell up in America and remain in England."

What did he expect her to say? He talked endlessly about the possibilities open to him for staying in America or settling permanently in England. She might not be a veteran of the war between men and women, but she wasn't stupid or insensitive either. Aunt Madge saw to that. From the first day she had set eyes on Alexander Barrington's friend, Madge had insisted Lear was falling in love with her. It was the last thing she wanted, and Jane made it a point never to show him anything but friendship. If he chose to think she was falling in love with him, he was sadly mistaken, and for that they both had Barrington to thank.

"I wish you a safe and pleasant journey, Mr. Lear," Jane said, moving quickly to take his hand and usher him out of the studio. "I know you must be anxious to depart, so we'll not keep you, shall we, Aunt Madge?"

From his perch high above the conservatory, James Manley watched Lear's short visit and was delighted. Madge and Lear's timing couldn't have been worse. He could make an educated guess about what must have happened. Peering through his high-powered lenses, he knew Jane was having difficulties just before they arrived over what looked like a drawing of Alex Barrington. He laughed at Jane's efforts to hide the picture, so he wasn't in the least surprised when she seemed unwilling to tolerate a long visit. He wished young Lear the best of luck, but he had also bet a small fortune the lad didn't have a chance. Manley couldn't remember when he had been so enthralled in the machinations of the human comedy or wanted so much to be thirty-five again. If he had met a Jane Daitry in his day, he would have known what to do to make her happy. But he had never met her like, and whose fault was that? His and his alone. He had spent his blunt on dancers and opera singers, had even gone on bended knee to the great Sarah Siddons herself, and there, for sure, he had caught cold. She very nearly laughed in his face.

He felt sorry for John Lear. With Alex in the picture, truly and figuratively, no other man had a chance. As for Barrington, he might be up on all that was going, but he was an idiot about women, judging by his famous affair with wild Clea Wesley.

Looking down on Jane again, he was happy to see that she went back to working on her picture of Alex with a very lovely smile on her face.

Chapter Thirteen

With Lear out of sight, Alex had no one to tell him what was going on in Jane Daitry's life.

He had dismissed her as a bluestocking, but the night of Rose Bellingham's party she was all go and game. At least he thought so at the time. But in the end she was none too pleased with him when he left her abruptly at Madge's side. He had sent masses of flowers, and had never heard a word. He would never know how Jane felt if Lear didn't get back soon.

And what about London's dandies? Why weren't they knocking down the doors to get to Jane and shepherd her about town? He looked hard enough, and still hadn't seen hide nor hair of Jane at the theater, balls, or routs he had attended on the chance he would see her. He saw enough of Madge Brooks. The woman was everywhere, but Lady Jane was not at her side. In fact, he hadn't set eyes on the Irish woman in weeks. Strange indeed.

He had done all he could. He had discharged his duty to Patrick, and should have been content and able to go forward on his work with the Legion without a thought to the obligation he felt toward the Daitrys.

But it didn't seem to be as easy as it should have been.

Alex longed to go to her studio, despite the fact he knew next to nothing about art. But he couldn't help being curious.

He would wait John Lear's return and ask him to get

permission to see Lady Jane's paintings when that lioness protector of hers was not about.

Content to wait until then, Alex called for his secretary to draft a letter to be sent to a list of retired officers and serving men who might assist him in finding jobs for his Legion. If he got the same enthusiasm he had received from his most intimate friends, his burgeoning organization would soon be on its way.

It was three o'clock in the morning. The air was crisp and cool, the stars so bright, so close above Alex felt he could touch them. He was feeling no pain after a late supper. He preferred to walk, after saying a slightly bibulous good-bye to several friends at Stephen's Hotel. Pleased with his day's work and a successful night at the gaming tables, Alex was whistling one of the latest music hall ballads when he saw tongues of firelight coming from the garden of a house in the square ahead.

He looked to see if help was on its way, didn't see another soul, and sprinted toward the house. In a few moments he was up and over the high brick wall at the back of the house, and moments later was sprawled flat on his back, blood oozing from a cut to the forehead. Alex groaned and tried to fend off the large hulk who had hit him and was now planning another assault.

"I'm the Earl of Trent come to see if there was a fire," he explained, bobbing out of the man's reach, trying to get to his feet.

Working in the studio, Jane heard the commotion and came running toward them.

"What is going on here?" she called into the darkness. The watchman raised his lantern, and Jane saw it was Alex. She knelt beside him to take his pulse, and her hand came away dripping blood. Alex laughed and handed her his handkerchief to staunch the blood. Jane made her voice hard.

"Why did you injure his lordship?" she asked the broad-shouldered man, who was still holding a cudgel.

"I'm Johnson, the nightwatchman, my lady," he said helplessly. "I thought he was a villain!"

He looked up at the window, hoping the old governor was still awake and would give him some help. At once the curtains parted, and with a candle lighting his face, Manley was signaling him to keep mum. Soon after, Rollins, Manley's valet, arrived breathless and cursing, unable to get his arm into a robe to cover his billowing nightshirt.

"Help me bring the gentleman into the house," the valet said to the watchman.

"No. Into the studio. There's a couch close by," Jane ordered. Alex, far from seriously wounded, felt humiliated.

"I've got a hard head. I can walk," he growled.

"Don't trouble yourself, my lady, I shall see to his lordship," the valet said.

"Nonsense. Rollins, you and the watchman can safely leave Lord Alexander with me," she stated. "Waken my maid, and tell her I will need hot water and bandages for his lordship's wound."

Forgetting his pique, Alex laughed, admiring Jane's savoir faire. He waited until the men left.

"It will do your reputation little good, if it comes out I spent time on your couch, my lady."

"I don't give a rap for my reputation," Jane said tartly. "You will never be a threat."

She knew she was lying through her teeth. He was very much a threat to her happiness. And if he knew, he could make mincemeat of her presumptions. Moreover, Aunt Madge would have a stroke. No, if she did not get Alex out of her studio immediately after she bandaged him, she would not speak for what might happen. It was more than flesh and blood could stand having him so close. Jane had never understood before why the poets rhapsodized over love and lust. She did not want to examine how she felt when Alex came too near.

"So this is your famous studio and the source of the fire I thought I saw two roads away," Alex chuckled. "It is like daylight here."

"And you were going to put out the fire, were you?" Jane asked, trying to keep a disinterested voice. "A bad bruise is what you get when you play the good citizen."

Alex feigned a moan. Much as his head ached, he wanted a good look around the studio. He was very impressed. The accommodations were fine, so unlike the disorder of the few studios he had seen before.

Somehow he was not surprised. The lady artists he knew drew nauseating pictures of broody cows, mincing shepherdesses, and all manner of nature he had never laid eyes on. His mother's artistic friends, male and female, talked art around the dining table, but he had seen none of their "great works," and, he suspected, neither had his mother.

Until this time, he had not felt a terrible lack in his education, and thus vowed to try and not say anything stupid. He suspected Jane would not take kindly to anyone making a fuss over her pictures, especially if one pretended knowledge that was false.

But whether she was a talented amateur or a gifted artist, Alex could see she worked at her trade. The studio was full of a variety of paintings, studies, exercises in oils, charcoal, watercolors, and pencil.

Soon the unwelcome arrival of Jane's maid carrying hot water and bandages, with James Manley behind her, brought an end to his investigation. He agreed to submit to Jane Daitry's ministrations, although the bleeding had long since stopped. She was gentleness itself. The wound was minor, and he refused to wear anything but the smallest bandage.

"Very gallant of you, dear boy," James Manley said,

admiring Jane's nursing skills. "My watchman is very worried."

"Please assure him I harbor no hard feelings. He was doing his job very well, I must say. The next time I want to see Lady Jane's work, I hope I shall be able to do so without getting my head bashed in," Alex said.

He wanted that permission very much.

"If Lady Jane approves, and you are very discreet, Barrington, I shall see that the rear door near the street is open and the watchman will permit you to enter," Manley said, not at all sure he was doing the right thing. Madge would ring a peal over his head if she knew, but somehow he didn't think anyone, least of all Jane, would tell her.

"I am sorry, but I do not like being observed when I work," Jane said. It was not what she wanted to say, but instead needed to say. She would get little accomplished with Alex's much too disturbing person anywhere about.

James Manley could not believe Jane was so poor-spirited as to send a man as attractive, as wealthy, and as eligible as Alexander Barrington away. Surely she could not be interested in John Lear over Alex? The idea shocked him.

Jane's refusal to permit Alex to visit her studio made the old man doubt the evidence of his own eyes or his very expensive spyglass. Why the hell was the girl always drawing Alex's picture if she did not want him about? There was no understanding women, and now he remembered why he had never married. There was no accounting for how a woman would behave when an attractive man crossed her path.

Alex stood up slowly, bowed over Jane's hand, and followed Manley out of the studio.

The old man felt every moment of his seventy-five years on earth, and no wiser than when he had entered it.

Chapter Fourteen

Major, Lord Alexander Barrington, had not been called a master military strategist for nothing. He was not about to be barred from Jane Daitry's studio as easily as she or Lord Manley seemed to think. In fact, asking permission to visit her studio was a polite digression the other night. But when Jane had effectively barred him entrance, he actually became quite determined to break down the barriers she was building around herself.

His campaign started slowly. He scoured the bookshelves of Ackermann's, Hatchard's, and Hookham's and ransacked his own and his mother's library for books on art and painters, then sent them one at a time to Jane. Her notes told of her gratitude, but did not offer to lift her ban on his visits to her studio.

Then he began sending her notices of gallery showings and the latest exhibits. She turned them down with the explanation that her work took precedence over everything. He had to believe that was true, because his own prowling about the town showed Jane must still be living a nun's sort of life. Obviously, the party at Lady Bellingham's was a rare exception.

Finally, one day he decided he was going about the matter all wrong and dropped in on his mother, the Countess of Trent, at teatime. His mother was a formidable, white-haired, arthritic woman with the widest possible interests.

"My darling Alex, how nice to see you," she greeted

him as the last of her guests departed. He gave her a big boyish grin. The sometimes dour, detached Earl of Trent was, here in her crowded drawing room, content to be a fond son.

"You were in the neighborhood, of course, and simply could not go another step without seeing your adored mother, correct?" Lady Irene laughed up at her beloved eldest child.

She was chiding him, and he loved her for it. He bent and kissed her wrinkled cheek and took a cup of tea from her.

"Darling mama, do you know Madge Brooks at all?" he asked casually and without preamble. His mother was a font of information, and had receptive ears as well as a coterie of friends who kept her well informed about the happenings of the *ton*.

"She likes me in spite of my wayward son, is the way she puts it," Lady Irene replied, studying Alex. She loved all three of her children, of course, but her daughter and younger son were well married and had lives of their own. It was left to Alex to do the family duty toward her. He seemed to do it gladly and with great good grace, and she counted herself lucky to have him so close by and unfailingly attentive.

"How do I worm my way into her affections?" Alex asked carefully. He didn't want to hint about his interest in Jane Daitry if he didn't have to. After all, he didn't understand himself what was happening to him, and, if asked, would be at a standstill to explain his sudden concern with the girl's welfare.

"Unbend that rigid code of silence of yours," his mother said quickly. The painful events surrounding Pamela Britton-Steen and Alex's old colonel were still fresh in her mind. That her son never wanted to put himself in the right, and cared less than a tinker's damn about how he was regarded by the *ton* was an ongoing issue between the two.

"What good would that do?"

"I haven't the foggiest. But if you want to turn her up sweet, you have to start someplace." Lady Irene wondered at Alex's strange request, but she knew better than to question him. Alex was like his father, very much his own man, and the way to keep his good opinion was to listen and wait for him to tell what he wanted her to know.

"I'll think about it, darling," he said. "And, Mama, what do you know about art?"

"Precious little. I know what I like, and that's the way I always bought my pictures. For all the money I spend, I have an indifferent collection" she laughed. Then with a twinkle in her faded blue eyes she added easily, "Now your friend Clea Wesley is reputed to be an expert, one of the best judges of paintings. Strange you didn't know that. I suppose you talk of other things."

Alex choked on the scone he was eating. Only his unconventional mother would refer to his mistress with a straight face and only the slightest bit of bawdiness. He loved her dearly for remarks like that, and often found her delightfully imperturbable in a troubled world. Alex finished his tea and bade his mother a warm farewell. He hated to think what life would be like without this rock of warm sympathy and good sense.

Of course, Clea was the one who could judge Jane's talents better than anyone else. Alex knew many people relied on her opinions before buying pictures, even though they might deplore the way she lived. How stupid of him not to have thought of her himself. But the truth of the matter was Clea no longer commanded his affections or his attention as she once did.

She was as fascinating as ever, always full of life, bright, and amusing, but in ways he knew from other love affairs, his interest had begun to dim. Long before he realized it, even before her husband had pleaded with her to be more circumspect, he had begun distancing himself from the ever-increasing romantic attention she demanded of him. Alex recognized all the signs. It was not the first time he had lost interest in a woman without apparent reason. And he was afraid it would not be the last. Love, of course, never entered into his affairs with women. They knew it from the first. His affair with Clea, while the longest in his career on the town, was purely physical. Clea was undeniably enchanting, and he took some comfort that when he had the courage to end the liaison very soon now, they would remain friends and no rancor would mar their mutual admiration. After all, Clea once confessed to him that she discarded men like underclothes, and boasted of her own fickle nature. She had left London soon after Lady Bellingham's party, and Alex reckoned that all this introspection was due to her absence.

However, he was not a man to give a woman a conge without his conscience revolting. He would buy Clea an indecently expensive bit of jewelry, and hope that she might sense his receding interest and dwindling ardor and, with her fierce pride, make the break before he needed to say anything unkind or hurtful. He would rather face a firing squad than the tears and scorn of a woman. He shuddered at what lay ahead.

Still, if he took his mother's advice and patched up his quarrel with Madge Brooks and got the Legion off the ground successfully, surely a halo would descend from the heavens and choke him.

"As usual, darling Mama, you are quite right on all your suggestions," Alex said, taking his leave. "I just need time to summon the courage to face Mrs. Brooks."

Chapter Fifteen

Jane paced the studio like a caged lion.

It was long after midnight, and all her brushes were perfectly clean, but she was still desperately in need of something to do with her hands. Ever since she had sent Alex to the roundabout, refusing to give him permission to visit her studio, her work had gone to seed. Piercing steel gray eyes and thick blond hair got in the way. They were the last images she saw before she threw herself into bed at night, and the first when she awoke.

Her new miniature of Alex lay unfinished, refusing to come to life, stale and dead in contrast to her earliest efforts. For the first time Jane was unable to concentrate and, worse, could not come up with new inspirations for the next picture needed for the portfolio. Jane had never been at a loss for the next subject, yet here she was in the most perfect studio any artist ever had, in the most exciting city in the world, paralyzed by inertia.

Sunk in gloom, Jane almost didn't hear the scratching at the door. Startled by the sound, she could hardly make out the figure of a man outside. The door opened, and she picked up a heavy piece of driftwood used sometimes to hold down her drawings.

Much to her surprise it was Alex Barrington in superbly cut black evening clothes and snow white linen. Jane didn't know what to say.

Alex's eyes were full of mischief, and laughter

creased the corners of his mouth. It was a perfect mouth, one she had drawn from memory so often she could almost feel it under her fingertips. Once that had been enough, but the more she saw of him, the more she wanted those lips on hers. The wantonness of her feelings shocked her, and she busied herself cleaning the palette.

She wouldn't fool herself into thinking that Alex had come to see her for herself. It was more than likely he was slightly the worse for wear after a long night of revelry, and he probably didn't want to go home. Nothing else would explain this unholy intrusion. She glanced quickly over her shoulder to be sure the miniature of him was safely covered. It was.

"Where is the watchman?" Jane asked. "Why didn't he stop you?"

"He's a very stout fellow, and I gave him my word I was here very briefly and meant you no harm," Alex said. "I was passing along and had an irresistible urge to pay you a call. You keep very bad hours, my lady."

"And you, my lord, can't seem to take no for an answer," she said with a shake of her head. For even though he was in a slightly drunken state, she welcomed him. Oh, how she welcomed him. Jane was certain she would give away the most intimate feelings she had for him. Thus she was grateful for the state he was in. Any beau of the town could read her like a book, and Alex Barrington sober was a practiced lover and connoisseur of women from what Patrick and Madge had told her.

Alex fell into the nearest chair, his tall black hat rolling off his head and landing at his feet. He made no effort to retrieve it. She picked up the hat and began brushing the silk with her sleeve.

"Ask me why I disregarded your expressed wishes to come and watch you work."

"I was about to mention it," Jane said wryly.

"I hate secrets and mysteries," he said, the words slurred. "Perhaps this wasn't the best idea, but I really am impossible when I'm told I can't do something."

Jane was the same, but she wouldn't admit it. She must keep up this pretense of disapproval, even though there was nothing more she wanted at that moment than to have Alex exactly where he was. In fact, she wanted Alex forever. There, she had said it to herself, and the realization echoed in her head and her heart and made her senses reel. It was her most impossible dream, on the same plane as her ambition to be a great miniaturist and painter. What a fool she was, wanting the moon, not content with the sun alone. Patrick once said her refusal to compromise would be her undoing. She didn't doubt it, but she was helpless to do otherwise.

Alex was watching Jane attack her brushes in agitation. It was obvious that something was irritating her. He watched in fascination. Her brow was furrowed, her dark hair carelessly pulled back into a chignon, her face devoid of any of the deceptions he knew women used to enhance their attractiveness. Her teeth bit into her lip. He had seen her do that the few times they had met, and he suspected she was not even aware she was doing it. He would remember to look for that mannerism later in their association. He was sure it meant beware, storm warnings on the horizon.

Yet again Alex noticed that Jane's face was not beautiful by the prevailing standards of the *ton*, but her magnificently arched eyebrows and slightly long aristocratic nose and blue violet eyes spoke of good breeding and a fiery independence. The more he saw her, the more he thought John Lear had chosen himself a formidable wife. His friend deserved the best, but could he manage such a firebrand? Jane Daitry, to his mind, would make an interesting, if not comfortable companion. He was glad he didn't have to contend with such a female.

"Well, tell me why you don't let anyone watch you at your easel," Alex persisted. "I know people who lounge about the Turner and Constable studios while they work. When Gainsborough painted my mother as a bride, she said it was more salon than atelier."

"How kind, if not foolhardy, of you to link my name with such masters," Jane said, her eyes roaming the studio. "There is nothing strange about disliking people looking over one's shoulder. Artists must have solitude, or at least I must."

"Are you certain it is not the fear of being thought an amateur and a bad artist?" he asked carelessly. He saw Jane bridle and could have kicked himself for not keeping his tongue between his teeth. They had arrived at a pleasant state. If she was not as friendly as he would have liked, she was not her usual acerbic self either.

Jane put down the brushes and wiped her hands on a cloth nearby.

"I think I may have stayed too long, Lady Jane," Alex said, at once sober. When was he going to learn that most people found his honesty and bluntness objectionable? Polite society, or women at least, were not the army, where a man was allowed to be himself. His regret at the loss of the life and career he loved was never keener. He often felt like a fish out of water.

Alex rose from the chair. He was far more tired than he realized. He stole a glance at the paintings he had hoped to study when he first came to the studio. He shrugged and saluted the stony figure standing at the door waiting for him to leave.

"I am sorry I offended you, Jane Daitry, and perhaps one day you will allow me to see your pictures," Alex said, suddenly weary and dispirited. "If you can believe it, I am interested in your career. I am sorry you feel you can't trust me."

Jane watched Alex, now fully sober, walk steadily toward the watchman, who was holding the garden door open for him. It took all her strength to keep from begging him to come back.

It was not the way Jane had wanted the evening to end. Far from it. There had been moments when she could dare hope that they were about to arrive on a new, equal footing. Then why in heaven's name did he feel it incumbent on him to question how she felt about people seeing her work? Of course, he was right . . . poisonously right . . . only she couldn't admit how little faith she had in her worth.

A man like Alexander Barrington, with his money, his impeccable lineage, his vast family lands, and his magnificent maleness had a secure place in life and never needed assurances of his worth. But she, Jane Daitry, of the near-bankrupt House of Craig, once high in the Irish nobility, and a descendent of depleted English stock, needed all the assurances she could get.

It wasn't enough to dedicate her life to becoming the best artist she could be, Jane was learning. She needed single-mindedness and a disregard for anything or anyone who stood in her way. Well, she had lost her way, led astray by a lithe, Greek god with gray eyes that would make a hole in any woman's heart. But not her heart, Jane promised. She would learn to be hard-skinned, single-minded, but practical as well. It was time she took the blinders off and fought for what she wanted. She would play by her own rules. She would put Alexander Barrington out of her mind. Having given her the first glimpse of what passion and love might be, he had taken over her mind and clouded the path she had chosen for herself. But she had lived without him and love for twenty-six years, and she would live without his shattering presence for many years to come.

But could she call that living, without someone as

vital as Alex, a small inner voice asked Jane as she blew out all the candles in the old greenhouse and made her way back to the house?

When tears began coursing down her face, she briskly brushed them aside. She had no time for stupid, missish sentiment. No time at all.

Chapter Sixteen

The Earl of Trent was a man torn by demons.

Now that he was fully engaged with a half dozen old army comrades in launching the Legion, Alex heard stories of starvation and neglect enough to drive him mad. He and his friends felt deeply that these men and their families deserved a better fate.

Alex worked at fever pitch, finding as many jobs as he and his small band could gather. Alex's brother Edward was combing his estates and houses for jobs. Even with his huge resources, Alex was ashamed of the relatively few positions he could find for his charges. That many of the men Alex sought to help were without trades made the task of finding employment doubly difficult.

He had wanted the advice of his friend and mentor, the much revered Captain Tarn Maitland, but he and his wife had been on a visit abroad with their five children and due back in London today.

Tarn Maitland had many business enterprises and would know how Alex could go about setting up small businesses and training the men. But meanwhile, the waiting made him restive.

Alex was so driven by his awakened sense of duty, that even his hard-bitten valet, Atkins, thought him slightly cracked on the subject.

"Ye have a good heart, sir, but many of those applying to you for assistance will take your blunt and show you the back of their heels," the stocky one-time batman protested.

Atkins was not the only one who warned him not to put too much store in the effort he was making, but Alex was not expecting all the men to be angels.

One of the few who gave him wholehearted support was John Lear, fresh from the country four days earlier. They were relaxing after breakfast at Lear's house, leased after his quarrel with Alex. It was an old, charming cottage not far from Hyde Park, and Lear was talking about buying it.

"I think this is the best thing that ever happened to you," Lear was saying, after giving Alex a handsome draft on his bank for Barrington's new organization. "Now that I have a residence in Yorkshire, I will ask my estate manager to see if he can use a few more willing hands about the place. If he does, I shall tell you."

Alex was feeling a great deal better since Lear's return. His friend looked more handsome, confident, and happier than Alex had ever seen him. Clearly his unrequited love for Colby Browning was a thing of the past.

"Your time in the country and your new properties have given you ruddy cheeks and the air of a man who has attained everything he could wish," Alex observed carefully. "Lady Jane and Mrs. Brooks must be making a great fuss over you. Dare one hope there will be news from that quarter?"

Alex was holding his breath. The question had been plaguing him since Lear had arrived back in London. Alex had to know. Had to.

Lear turned red and replenished the glasses in front of them before replying. "I can't imagine what you mean."

Lear was not a man to play silly buggers about something so important, and Alex felt able to take a shallow breath and ask further.

"Really, John? No news of a marital nature?"

"Frankly, Alex, I don't know how I feel. And since Lady Jane is not a romantic, I am afraid we have progressed very little, if at all, from the first day we met."

Alex looked to see if Lear was suffering from this state of uncertainty. Thankfully his friend, from what Alex could tell in his subversive scrutiny, seemed as cheerful as ever.

Quite suddenly, the twin demons looked less black. Tarn Maitland was home, and Alex had an appointment with him in a few hours. Matters would move swiftly now. The miserable ending to the evening in Jane's studio had oppressed Alex for weeks. But with Lear returned to the scene, perhaps he could make amends for his boorishness. He didn't want to look too closely at the airy feeling that was overtaking him. What he did acknowledge was that his curiosity about Jane Daitry was as keen as ever. That was as far as he chose to go in the matter of introspection.

"I say, I think it is about time that I made some effort to erase Mrs. Brooks's dislike of me and sampled some of James Manley's fine Madeira again." Alex hoped he was a better actor than he sounded.

Lear was startled. "What has happened to you since I left, Alex? Are *you* intending to apologize to the old dragon?"

"Surely you believe, as I do, that we should be the official escorts for Lady Jane and introduce her to the opera, theater, and the galleries where an artist should be seen," Alex went on cheerfully. "It wants a strong push from Manley, his sister, and the two of us to insure that the Lady Jane sees what she is missing."

"I'll bet you a monkey you can't change Lady Jane's attitude toward such frivolities."

"I'll stake you a thousand pounds against any paltry sum you say," Alex replied jauntily, trying not to sound like a cheeky barrow boy with his first sovereign in his pocket. Actually, he wasn't in the least certain that he could get Madge Brooks to give him house room, much less accept his apology, but it was worth anything to Alex to get back in Jane's good graces. Alex didn't want to examine too closely why it was so important to him to overcome Jane Daitry's aversion, but he meant to obtain her good opinion of him at all costs.

Was it because he couldn't abide having a woman so indifferent to him? Was he so overcome with the power of his own charms that his ego was bruised? These were lowering possibilities, especially since he prided himself as being above such false vanity. Alex quickly turned his mind elsewhere.

"I say, John, are you game for a good bruising ride up to Hampstead Heath and a pint at the Spaniards?" Alex asked. "It's a lovely day, and I need the exercise."

Lear fell in with the plan at once. As students at Oxford, in London for a lark, he and Alex often roamed the heath and stopped at the picturesque tavern, once a haunt of smugglers. It was welcome exercise when they needed a breather from the smoky city and its parties and late-night diversions.

Alex would have been very pleased with himself if he knew that at the very moment he had made his bet with Lear, Jane was taking copious notes and making sketches from an old folio of Italian masters he had found in his father's library and had delivered to her. From what he could decipher in the margins of his father's difficult script, the work was one of many he had bought on his grand tour. Alex hoped that the folio would go a way toward making amends for the night in the studio. What he got for his pains was a cryptic note saying she thanked him for his latest gift, but she could not keep it. She would return it as soon as she had finished making copies.

Now, as she labored over Alex's gift, laid out on the red carpet of the dais, Jane was lost to the present and transported by the talents of Michelangelo, Correggio, and Titian, genius she could never aspire to herself. Jane dropped her charcoal and covered her face with her hands. Tears as scalding as fire rained down her face and through her fingers. Her heart was cold, her senses reeling under the certainty of her limitations. She was being punished for her arrogance, and she threw herself down on the carpet and wept until she could weep no more.

High above, James Manley pushed aside his spyglass, shattered by the sight of Jane's suffering. He had no idea what troubled her, but he would find out and move heaven and earth to help her. He wanted to comfort her, but knew Jane would not appreciate being seen to such disadvantage. He waited a few moments, and then summoned his butler.

"My compliments to Lady Jane, and ask her if she would like to accompany me to Hyde Park."

Barrett stared at his master. He couldn't remember the last time Lord James had bestirred himself to be seen with the rest of the *ton* in Hyde Park at five. The old servant was delighted to convey the invitation to the young lady, but stopped at the doorway.

"But are you sure, sir, the young lady will want to be disturbed at all?" he asked.

His employer did a very strange thing indeed. He handed over his spyglass. The butler peered through it closely, saw what his lordship wanted him to see, and was equally concerned.

"She needs something to cheer her up, Barrett. Do we need a better reason?" Manley asked.

"No, sir. But I shall use the excuse of the post to explain why I am interrupting her. I've noticed she is always cheered when she hears from Ireland."

Chapter Seventeen

The Manley butler was well off the mark when he said Jane would be pleased to hear from Patrick, but he was right in that it offered a distraction.

Jane accepted the letters, hiding her face from him. Reading between the lines, Jane sensed that matters were more dire than before she left.

Jane was hardly surprised. She had always served to deflect the worst of Verna's storms at Daitry Hall. Now without her, poor Patrick had no one to shield him from Verna's sulfuric temper or to share his misery. The root of everything was money. Verna's father, contemplating marriage to a young widow, was threatening to change both his will and Verna's marriage portion. It appeared that Mike Byrne's solicitors had anticipated the circumstances and had drawn the settlements accordingly. Neither Patrick nor Verna had suspected Mike Byrne's cunning, and were now to pay dearly for their misplaced faith.

"Verna wants to go to law for relief," Patrick wrote. "But barristers and law courts cost money, and we are acutely short at the moment."

Jane detected Verna's influence in the wording. She obviously had pushed Patrick to ask for whatever money was left of the 500 pounds they had given her.

The butler coughed politely.

"His lordship will be wanting a reply, my lady," he said gently, calling attention to himself and his master's request that she join him later for a ride in the park. Jane had very nearly forgotten he was standing by. "Mrs. Brook's visit to Bath this past week has made him very lonely."

"Tell Lord James I will be happy to join him," Jane replied, smiling in apology for her lapse. "Please ask my maid to prepare my clothes." Jane turned back to her easel and began the finishing touches on preliminary sketches for a portrait of Madge Brooks, searching desperately in her mind for a solution to Patrick's worries. She had more than half the money she had left Ireland with and would post it back to Patrick immediately, but that was hardly all he needed.

Furthermore, sending most of her money back would leave her stone broke and unable to pay for the lessons she was determined to have. Where was she going to get money other than from her work? But was she good enough? Would people want her poor pictures when there was an army of more capable men and a lesser number of women geniuses, starving to death for lack of patronage?

After all the years hiding away and refusing to paint for money, the problem would now be selling herself. Jane groaned and applied herself vigorously to her work. Pretty and flattering pictures would have to emerge from her paints and pencils at a great rate if she was to help Patrick and herself. This was no time to worry about bastardizing her work. In one stroke the arrogance and misplaced pride were luxuries of the past. No more playing at being a painter above the fray and commercial need. How could she have fooled herself all these years? Who did she think she was?

Later, when she was ready to join James Manley in his carriage, she was no longer in shock, but somehow, and against all odds, she felt a new determination coursing through her. She had spent the intervening hours walking about the studio with a hard and merciless eye, studying the body of work she had done since coming to London, concluding bitterly she had a small but limited and possibly marketable skill. Her portraits were studies and nothing more. They were the most natural for her at this stage of her life. Always at the back of her mind was the idea of becoming a fine miniaturist. Nothing less would do.

It was a measure of her new resolve that Jane rushed to be dressed and ready for the butler's summons to meet James Manley. Until today she had steadfastly refused all invitations to leave her work during the day, on the grounds that she could not play at being a London gadabout. Now she needed to see and be seen everywhere, and the park at this hour was as good a place as any.

And what she saw while sitting and facing a beaming, happy James Manley in his ancient landau became a balm to her eye and made her hands itch to transfer the scene to canvas. She bitterly regretted her former intransigence, denying herself the sight of so much color and grace played against the pastel beauty that made Hyde Park such a magnet for society. She was happily taken by the splendid-looking men in the latest sartorial rage, or so her host hastened to tell her, of blue coats with brass buttons, leather breeches, and top boots made to shine with generous and vigorous applications of champagne, as decreed by Brummel himself.

Perched atop priceless cattle or tooling along in a stunning variety of brilliant carriages, the like of which could not be mustered anywhere else in the world, the males of the species were as disdainful, proud, and peacockish as their women. Ladies of certain and uncertain age preened on foot or in such carriages as made them visible for all to see, wearing sprigged muslin and silks, and hats from the most beautiful of milliner's confections to some that defied the laws of gravity and good taste. Anything that attracted attention was desirable, it seemed to Jane, herself arrayed in a simple dress of lavender silk and a corn-colored straw bonnet.

After the morning's emotional buffeting, the late-afternoon sun was warm and comforting, and Jane chose to luxuriate against the pearl gray leather of James Manley's carriage. She was tired, worn to the nub. She closed her eyes, pressing her gloved hands against her eyes.

"You work too much, my dear," James Manley said, his concern all too apparent. "I may have retired from the world—prematurely as it turns out—but I am not without experience. Let me help you."

Jane opened her eyes and looked at him.

"Please, Jane, don't say, 'I can't imagine what you mean,'" he said, giving a good imitation of Jane at her haughtiest. "Something is troubling you, and I wish to help."

Jane laughed in spite of herself. She wasn't a very good actress.

"I had a letter from Patrick," she said slowly, hating to reveal the most current disaster and state of Daitry finances. "I think perhaps it is time to stop playing at painting and start making it pay."

"Jane, I have more money . . . "

"Stop, please, Uncle James," Jane pleaded. "You know we will not accept anything. Where I will accept your help is advice on getting patrons, presupposing anyone will take me seriously."

"I rather think the two men approaching us could give you better guidance than I," Manley said eagerly, pointing behind her.

From the lather on their horses, Alex Barrington and John Lear had been riding hard. They tipped their hats and came to the Manley landau.

Two more handsome men could hardly be found in the park.

"How splendid of you to get Lady Jane away from her studio," Lear called out.

"What bribe did you use?" Alex asked, smiling down on the pair. He had seldom seen her in the daylight. Sunlight showed Jane to advantage. Her blue-black hair, startling eyes, and ivory complexion sparkled in natural light and added to her quiet dignity. But on a closer look he noticed a weariness about the eyes, a slight furrow above the nose, and a dispiriting slump to the shoulders that disturbed him. He had an almost uncontrollable urge to smooth away the furrow, wipe away the weariness.

At once Alex didn't want to understand what made him see Jane Daitry not as Patrick's sister, not as the future bride of his best friend, but as a woman who needed whatever comfort he could give her. Alex shook his head. He hadn't had a woman in weeks, not since Clea had taken off for the country to play, however reluctantly, the fond mother at the estate of her daughter's apparent husband-to-be. *Clea come back*, Alex pleaded silently. *I am having dangerous delusions*.

For her part, Jane was concerned that her heart would show in her eyes if she wasn't careful. It seemed an age since she had last seen Alex, and she prayed she didn't give anything. There was no use lying to herself. She wanted Alex beside her always, she wanted to know how it would feel with his arms around her, and other things she could only wonder about in her abysmal ignorance of what men and women did behind bedroom doors. Having Alex so near was too threatening, too painful.

"Give the reins to my tiger and join us," James Manley called out over the noise all around them. "We'll ride together for a while"

Jane was in turmoil. With little experience in the art of hiding her feelings, it was one thing to see Alex from a distance, but another to sit beside him or across the way. The carriage was large, but not large enough.

The transfer was soon accomplished, and Alex sat next to her. The heat rising from her loins made Jane move in her seat and made her breath shallow. She wanted to run and hide. She couldn't keep her eyes from wandering to the skin tight, fawn riding breeches he wore and the sight of thigh muscles straining against the cloth, reminding her of Michelangelo's statue of David she had copied so painstakingly from the book Alex had given her. She itched to feel the muscle and sinew beneath her fingers in the way she had imagined a sculptor must feel when he kneaded and molded his figures into life. Jane felt a line of perspiration forming above her lip, afraid to wipe it away, but more afraid one of the men would notice and understand her discomfort.

"I say, gentlemen, I have persuaded Lady Jane that it is about time she took commissions to paint portraits for a few people," Manley said glibly, "starting with me and my sister, of course."

Jane was dumbfounded. In one master stroke, James Manley had taken all the onus off the commercialism of her need to make money and had provided a way for people to judge her without delay. With her preliminary work for the portraits of brother and sister very near completion and done with love and care, she would feel less fearful of disapproval. They were the best she'd ever done.

She, least of all, thought her work outstanding, but knew it was not amateurish either. Each day she saw improvement in her skills. Now, with the crying need to send Patrick money, reality made painting no longer a private pleasure, but a new way of life. Jane couldn't embrace practicality willingly, but she wouldn't run away from it either. She straightened her back and clenched her fists. She would do what she had to do, no matter what, to achieve her aims. Better artists than she scrambled for money and recognition, and so would she. The goal was still intact. With enough money for Patrick and enough to pay a master for lessons, one day she would be a miniaturist and she would be happy to return to Ireland a success in front of the world.

"How wonderful. Will you start with one of me for my new house?" John Lear offered at once.

Alex was angry with himself for letting John steal a march on him, but he recovered quickly.

"I think that is a wise decision, and you must allow Mr. Lear and me to introduce you to the people in society who will become your sitters," Alex said smoothly. In his mind he ticked off likely subjects for her brush. "It is too late for you to appear in this year's Royal Academy exhibit, but you must allow us to take you to Somerset House to see the exhibit which I am told has 400 new pictures this year. You must meet influential people, and enter next year's show."

"I quite agree, Barrington, but first you must make your peace with my sister," Lord James chuckled. "She will be back from Bath in a few days."

"Indeed, I intended to go hat in hand to the good lady, although first we must have assurances from Lady Jane that she will permit us to be her official escorts."

Alex turned to Jane and caught her eye, then smiled in such an intimate and fond way that she very nearly melted in his arms. She had never been so close to Alex before.

James Manley noticed the flush on Jane's face, knowing it was due to Alex's marked attentions. Curious, he looked over at John Lear to see if that sterling young man saw the telling signs he did, but he was in a world of his own. Only a fool would sit idly by when a man like Alex Barrington was allowed full and unhampered range for his legendary charm.

Manley laughed to himself. He had always loved intrigue, and he was looking forward to what he hoped would be a very diverting and interesting few weeks ahead. If nothing else, his lovely Jane might be the center of the attentions of two very good men, and no woman, even one as dedicated to her painting as his unofficial ward, could fail to be flattered by the play unfolding for all of them.

Chapter Eighteen

"James, what do you make of this?" Madge Brooks strode into the library. "I have a note from Alexander Barrington asking permission to call on me."

"Well, that's an interesting turnup, I must say." He was lying through his teeth, and enjoying every minute.

"Should I receive him?" she asked, so unlike her usual decisive self.

"If you don't see him, I will," Manley responded. "Now, what does Alex say?"

"He sent lovely flowers and the message, I just told you. He will be here tomorrow, unless I refuse to see him. I can't give him the cut direct, can I?"

At five to three the next day, Alex slowed his steps one hundred yards from Manley's house, a furious argument going on in his head. Whatever possessed him to take a freakish interest in a woman who liked to paint and couldn't stand the sight of him? And if Madge Brooks threw him out on his ear, he deserved it.

He reached Manley's door with more trepidation than when he had faced the enemy in any of his battles under Wellington's command, and moved quickly before he could change his mind. Then the door swung open, seemingly in expectation of his visit, and the decision was taken out of his hands. He saw himself in Mrs. Brooks's presence, feeling once again like the Eton schoolboy unprepared for a Latin translation.

Madge directed him to an uncomfortable straight-backed chair and pointedly took a far more comfortable one. She ordered rataffia water for herself and Madeira for Alex. She was nothing less than an iceberg.

"Now, my lord, let us not waste each other's time," she said, not at all pleased that this enormously attractive man made her want to pat the back of her hair and wish she were thirty years younger. She might disapprove of his reputation, but she was female enough to acknowledge what other women saw to admire in the intensely virile Adonis across from her. "Let me know your reasons for calling on me."

Alex had tried out several means of approach, and discarded all of them, choosing the most direct.

"My wish, Mrs. Brooks, is to be as much help to Lady Jane as I can be," he said simply. "I believe that with your support, Mr. John Lear and I can help Lady Jane socially and further her career as an artist at the same time."

Madge Brooks's beringed and gnarled fingers clenched in barely concealed annoyance.

"Let us not play games with each other, my lord. I dislike you in general, and this painting madness that has overtaken Lady Jane, specifically," she said witheringly. "I will have no part in making Jane Daitry a figure of ridicule. It was not why I engaged to give her a season in London, and I believe Patrick Daitry will agree with my feelings."

"But if Lady Jane attracts the attention of eligible men, painting for money will not be necessary," Alex said mildly.

"I think that matter is happily accomplished," she interrupted airily. "My brother and I are sure her brother will second a certain gentleman's aspirations. Lady Jane will soon not need to paint for a living."

So matters were settled in that quarter, Alex realized. How odd that John hadn't told him. Only last night the two had shared a late supper at White's. Very curious indeed.

"I congratulate you, Mrs. Brooks, on the successful conclusion to your kind and generous efforts on behalf of the lady," Alex said, standing up, anxious to be away at once. "John Lear is a very good man, and I must congratulate him on capturing so great a prize."

Madge Brooks beamed, making no secret of the pleasure she took in her conduct of the interview and the wonderful news she had imparted. It made no difference to her that she was premature. Looking triumphant, she rose from her chair and summoned the butler.

Feeling inexplicably worn down and discouraged, Alex waited in silence for a servant to come and fetch him. Then a terrible anger suddenly rose in him, and he turned toward his hostess.

"I think, madam, it is time that at least one of your prejudices against me is explained," Alex said, his deep baritone low and harsh. "I was not and am not the ogre you and your friends, the Britton-Steens, think me for making their daughter pregnant. The man responsible was a friend of the family, whose name I will not tell you. I never offered for Pamela Britton-Steen, because we detested each other from childhood and I would not be gulled into a hateful marriage. If that makes me a rotter, so be it."

Disgusted with himself for allowing his pride to force him into a childish need to explain himself to this autocratic busybody, Alex turned on his heel and began striding out the room.

"How dare you slander that innocent girl?"

"I think, my dear, you are off the mark," James Manley said, appearing in the doorway and blocking Alex's way. "Forgive me for being blunt but Pamela was a whore then, and is today. I think you owe Lord Alexander an apology."

Madge Brooks stared at her brother in disbelief.

"How dare you use such language in my presence," she sputtered.

"I should have told you the truth years ago," Manley went on. "She was a disgrace. She would lie down with anyone. There is something else you ought to know, my dear. Our guest was more than just a brave soldier. He was a patriot when he sacrificed his brilliant career in the army. It's a pity he will not tell you the truth. I would tell you, but Wellington asked me to keep the matter a secret."

Shaken, afraid that Manley would say too much in his defense, Alex stood between brother and sister. He didn't want Manley to say more. There were things about the army debacle that needed to stay secret.

"I do believe, sir, that Mrs. Brooks need not be burdened with more today," Alex insisted before turning to bid Madge Brooks adieu. He smiled in his most engaging way. "I should be most grateful, madam, if you would forget all Lord James and I have said. It is history of no good to any of the people involved."

Her lined face red with embarrassment, Madge laid a restraining hand on Alex's arm and smiled shyly at him.

"I suppose I should not have listened to all the hateful gossip."

It was as close to an apology as she could allow herself, but that was even more than Alex had expected when he had embarked on gaining her favor. He smiled again, shook Manley's hand, and was away at once.

The old man waited impatiently until the door closed to confront his sister.

"What was that tarradiddle about Jane marrying Lear," he said angrily. "Is there something I don't know?"

Madge laughed. "It is just a matter of days, even hours, before he comes up to scratch," she assured him smugly.

"But he hasn't already?" Manley asked, holding his breath.

"I will not say yea or nay," she said, her eyes smiling. "I know you secretly prefer the Earl of Trent because he reminds you of your wild salad days, but I will not have him making overtures to our Jane. For all his protestations of innocence with Pamela Britton-Steen, he will never do for Jane. She needs a simple and compliant husband. John does not expect a chatelaine, or something equally grand, and that is what Alex's mother will want for a daughter-in-law."

"Madge, I will never forgive you if you force Jane into a marriage she doesn't want with a man she cannot love," he said, exasperated. "You have entirely too much influence on her."

Madge shrugged her ample shoulders and quit the room without another word.

Dejected, Manley sat resting his chin on the curved ivory handle of his walking stick. What a tangle. In many ways his sister was far more devious than he was in such matters and surely saw the world as it was, and not as he hoped it would be.

Chapter Nineteen

Alex Barrington scoured the London clubs looking for Lear. He couldn't understand nor did he want to understand why the marriage he had promoted with great guile should suddenly throw him into a state.

Alex arrived at White's, trying to convince himself he had no other reason to pursue Lear so assiduously, except to close the books on his responsibility to Patrick Daitry.

After all, he was scheduled to go to Scotland for a fishing party at "Fire" Burner's highland castle. It was an annual male party that brought ten of his oldest school and army friends together for an orgy of drinking, sport, and endless hours of good male talk. Alex cherished the trek. Even during his years fighting Boney, several times he had managed to secure leave, interludes in the fighting that had kept him sane. The fishing was legendary, and the cold, clear air and company of lifelong cronies always returned him to duty or London refreshed and ready to take up life again.

This year he needed Fire's Scottish fastness more than at any time, and he wanted to go with all the loose ends of his life tied up. Jane Daitry's future was the most important loose end.

How had the once irritating Lady Jane Daitry, at first an inconvenient obligation, become, almost without his realizing it, so much more to him, more than he wanted in fact? Without lifting her paint-smeared fingers, the midnight blue eyes and willowy figure occupied his thoughts more than any woman he had known in years. Even Clea, at the height of his passion for her, had never occupied his mind so much.

Once the banns were read, he would be able to go on with his work for his men and be reasonably satisfied. Once in the brisk country air, with the salmon running in the cold, clear dawn of a morning, he'd find, as he always did, a measure of contentment.

Alex beckoned to a club servant and ordered a large whiskey before dragging himself home. Once there, Atkins handed him several letters. On top was one on Lear's stationery.

> "Dear Alex:
> My father has taken ill, and I am on my way home. I shall write as soon as I can. Please call on Lady Jane."

A wave of mixed emotions overtook Alex. Concern for John, who was unusually close to his gentle, scholarly father, and happiness at being able to fulfill John's care of Jane. The other letter was from Madge Brooks.

> "My dear sir:
> After our conversation this afternoon, I am persuaded that I was ill-informed of your true character, and, in consultation with my brother, I am pleased to say our door is open to you whenever you wish to visit."

Alex could hardly credit it. There had been little indication when he had left the Manley house that the good lady had changed her mind about him. The day was full of surprises, and Alex didn't know if he was on his head or his knees.

Of one thing he was sure. The less he saw of Jane Daitry, the better. He reached for the rest of his mail, smiling at once at the sight and smell of a missive obviously from Clea. She was back from the country and full of news about her daughter's coming nuptials. She was to be at the Wingates' party and expected to see him there.

"We shall be discreet for a bit more time, but not too discreet!"

Chapter Twenty

Jane put aside her battered palette and wiped her hands on a paint-splattered cloth. She took a dozen steps back to examine the study of Madge she had completed at breakneck speed.

She hated clichés. They were home truths that made her angry. But in her case necessity was indeed the mother of invention, she agreed as her anxious eyes narrowed and flew over the surface of the work still wet and thick with paint.

She saw places that were amateurish and failed to capture the clear vision of what she had wanted when she was working, but all in all she wasn't completely ashamed of the results. *All this will be academic once I study with a master miniaturist and learn my craft.* Jane was convinced she had a skill there that far outdistanced her other efforts. For her, nirvana would be attained when she worked on miniatures, and if her results were not as fine, they were at least as creditable as the early efforts of Richard and Maria Cosway or Andrew Robertson and the rest of her gods.

"It's brilliant," John Lear called out from the doorway.

Jane knew she should be pleased by his praise, but she was merely amused and then irritated. He barely glanced at the portrait again when he came into the studio. She knew her art bored him to tears, as it seemed to do with everyone else. Instead he watched her with admiring eyes, as he always did.

"I had a note this morning that my father has had one of his spells. I am hurrying to Yorkshire to be with him," Lear said in a rush.

Jane turned, suddenly seized with panic. His eyes were filled with hunger.

"Darling, Jane."

"Please don't go on," she pleaded. Once the words were out she knew she would have to hurt him. No matter how well phrased, she was going to have to refuse him, and he didn't deserve to be made unhappy. Even in her limited experience, she knew there were few men she would meet who would be as good and loving. But he could never have her heart. Fool that she was, that had long since been the property of someone who didn't want it and needed nothing from her.

"Let me speak. I want to take care of you. I know you don't love me, but I will be patient. Can't you send me on my painful journey with some happy expectation?"

Oh, why did he have to say that? How could she be cruel to him at this particular time and make him even more unhappy? Time enough when he returned from the country to make him understand.

"Please, don't ask me for an answer now."

Lear beamed and made to take Jane in his arms, something he had wanted to do almost from the first day they met. He was entranced by her, but he had never felt certain she returned his feelings. He dared not ask for more for she had not turned him down out of hand. Time would settle matters, but for the moment he would be content.

Jane allowed him to hold her hand for a brief moment, but could not return his embrace. She hated the charade she was forced to play.

She stepped back, ashamed to have allowed herself to be less than honest. Much as she yearned to have a man's arms around her, they could never be John

Lear's arms. Never. He deserved to be cherished and loved, but not by her, and very soon she would have to tell him so.

John sensed her withdrawal and put it down to her fastidiousness, but perhaps not just that alone. He had done what he had never dared do before—interrupt her work—and she was anxious to get back to it. He would try to be patient and console himself with the knowledge that other women had been devoted to painting before marriage, but settled down afterward. Her work was charming and laudable, but only for the moment, because she needed to make money. In time, he would go to Ireland with Jane to see how he could help Patrick and relieve her mind of worry.

"I hope you find good news at the end of your journey," she said, eager to end the painful interview before honesty made her tell him the truth and wipe away the happy expression on his pleasant face.

John had been of two minds about offering for her before he left for Yorkshire, but seeing her again after a few days' absence had made him anxious to push his suit. He'd been prepared for a less happy result, and while he would have preferred a more enthusiastic assurance, on the whole matters had gone well.

He kissed her hand and left at once.

Chapter Twenty-one

The Wingate masquerade party was well launched, lubricated with shiploads of champagne when Alex arrived at one o'clock, a menacing, one-eyed, bearded pirate with a lethal dirk in his waistband.

He barely made his presence known to his hosts when Marie Antoinette took his arm and led him off without a word to a side room. The door was hardly closed when Clea Wesley threw herself into Alex's arms, pressing her half-bared breasts against him, insinuating her legs between his, hungrily exploring his mouth with her tongue sliding her hands down the back of his tight breeches.

He attempted to hold her off.

"Give me a chance to catch my breath," he pleaded. For the first time since he and Clea had become lovers, her blatant desire for him couldn't touch off a passionate response.

"Alex, you don't know how much I needed you," she murmured, heedless to his withdrawal. She put her head against his chest. "It's so hard to be good surrounded by pious elegance."

He laughed, only this time it was false. He didn't know how to hide his sudden disgust of the way she played the wanton, her hands greedy to arouse a need in him to match her own. He moved away and walked across the room to try to find a way to defuse her ardor and try to understand his own coldness. Seldom had he wanted to withstand Clea and her demands. It was a puzzle, and not a pleasant one.

Besides, it was no time for Clea to play her usual sport in this room. They both knew from past occasions that it would soon be invaded by others bent on the same game. He moved to lock the door.

Clea took it as a sign that Alex was as eager as she and took his hand to drag him to the settee across the room.

"No, Clea. Your daughter is only affianced, not married to the duke's family," Alex said, trying his best not to hurt her with a rank refusal to make love to her. "Moreover it's the talk of the clubs that your husband is a serious contender for high office."

The truth was Alex hadn't heard a word about Stuart Wesley's chances for high office anywhere or cared one way or the other, but the man's naked ambitions gave him a heaven-sent way out of an affair that had died.

Now the unpleasant task before him was telling Clea the truth. He hated the end of an affair, whatever the cause. It was a death of hope over experience. He was not a man to give his heart away and, worse, love one woman. He had no excuse, no reason for this, and he sometimes envied his friends who found women that meant everything to them. He longed to lose himself in love, but it had never happened, and he was afraid it never would.

"Alex, didn't you miss me?"

He looked over at Clea. All at once she was not the brazen, fearless hoyden who had led him and so many others on a merry hunt for new thrills. She had given him hours of pleasure and chased his army blue-devils to the farthest corners of his mind. What he saw instead was a woman dreading, as he did, the bleak years ahead, loss of hope, and naked disillusionment. Her usual lively brown eyes and her mouth were drawn and weary at the edges. He had seen Clea, when she thought his attention was elsewhere, examining the lines of aging, hating daily reminders of the swift passage of time. Would she see in his eyes confirmation, not of the end of passion, but of the coming of middle age? He hoped not.

What drove him away was Jane Daitry. Alex didn't have the heart to confirm her dread, not now at least. He crossed the room to take her in his arms and give them each brief respite from the truth and the world.

Toward dawn, Alex found himself wandering aimlessly about the town, or was it aimless? It didn't surprise him in the least when he came upon the back of Manley House, drawn by the lights in Jane's studio and his own need to see her again.

He took a few stones and flung them easily over the wall. It was his signal to the watchman. The door opened at once.

A guinea changed hands, and Alex was at the studio in a long stride. He opened the door and looked in. Jane was fast asleep in a chair next to the easel, looking younger and more vulnerable than he had ever noticed, so wonderfully appealing that his heart turned over. Alex felt like an intruder, and yet he couldn't move. His eyes fastened like a magnet on the thick black hair that could never seem to stay bound. He looked away quickly. It would not do to dwell on her overly long in such an unguarded moment. Jane's long, slim hands, never still when she was awake, rested quietly in her lap, as if exhausted.

Rooted to the spot, Alex knew he should withdraw as quietly as he had come, but he couldn't move. He wanted more than anything to gather Jane in his arms and cradle her against him and still the occasional flutter of her transparent eyelids, dark from exhaustion. Jane was far from enjoying the deep and refreshing sleep she needed, and that disturbed him more than anything.

Alex turned away, afraid he would be driven to do something unforgivable. Two women drew on his sympathy tonight, and he liked the feeling it gave him. Was he, after all, human?

"How long have you been here?" Jane called sleepily as he turned to leave.

"Not long," he replied.

"What brought you so late, or do I mean early?" she said, squinting up at the carriage clock. Then she saw the costume under his cape. "What are you dressed for?"

Alex looked down at his white silk shirt opened to the waist and high boots polished to mirror sheen, and laughed at the spectacle he made.

"Surely there are more important pursuits for you and your idle friends than dressing up like a pack of children bored with twisting cats' tails?"

At first Alex bridled at her jibe, and then remembered Jane was only saying what he had thought himself near the end of the evening when the drooping headdresses of old women dressed like Cleopatra and thick-set fellows dressed as Romeo or Caesar, sagging in the middle, assailed him as he left. Those few parties he chose to attend seemed fine in the early hours, but by the time he was ready to leave, he wondered why he'd bothered. How like Jane, with her clear sight, to see the ridiculousness of it all.

"You do have a way with words," Alex replied, annoyed with himself, knowing he deplored the waste of his time and yet was doing nothing to change his ways. He was even more annoyed that it took this long-limbed, black-haired hellion to make him face himself. He wrapped his cloak tighter. "You make me feel like a fool."

Jane was instantly sorry. "I have a way of speaking like a prig," she said, moving toward the tea table. "It really is none of my affair how people comport themselves. I shouldn't judge things so harshly."

"I was going to say you have an unerring gift for making me feel three feet tall sometimes. But let us have a truce."

Jane agreed at once, although she couldn't imagine how anyone, much less she, could diminish the mighty Earl of Trent in any way.

"I gladly accept whatever terms for a truce you offer," she said, looking at him with new eyes, no less loving. This first sign of vulnerability he was capable of made her warm toward him as never before. "Will you join me in a dish of tea?"

Alex agreed eagerly, although puzzled by a new tone in her voice and a curious look in her deeply lashed, blue eyes. He stood next to her and watched the way her long, strong fingers managed the homey ceremony of warming the brown earthen teapot, measuring out the tea, and arranging the shortbread on a plain, white plate.

Unbidden, Alex could picture Jane presiding over his family's heirloom silver service, surrounded by tiers of cakes and sandwiches, jellies and jams. He saw Jane presiding over the gold-and-white drawing room of Clairmont, his favorite house and the family seat.

Alex moved as if stung. He didn't like the errant drift of his mind. What was he thinking? Damn it, she was promised to his best friend, and a better prospect for a husband never lived.

"Milk or lemon?" Jane was asking.

"Milk." He would drink his tea and be off as soon as possible. Tired and dispirited after his encounter with Clea was the only explanation he could think of for the way his mind was working. Jane Daitry didn't need him any more than he needed her. He'd give her a wide berth after tonight. And if Madge Brooks held him to his offer to escort them about the town, he would do so until it was time to leave for Scotland, and this mad fantasy would die aborning, as it should.

"You are very pensive, my lord," she said, smiling at the awkward pause that overtook them.

"I think it is time we became Jane and Alex," he said, suddenly wanting desperately to hear his name on her lips.

"It would be a very great breach of manners, most inappropriate, sir," Jane said shyly. "And very difficult."

"And why is that?"

"The fact is, for so long you were this mythic figure rescuing my brother from the natural high spirits of a young officer, saving his life, and bringing him home at your expense. You were unreal, and that is the truth."

"No wonder you took such an instant dislike of me in Ireland, and don't say you didn't." Alex laughed.

"Yes, I did, but that was because you were so remote, so disdainful that you didn't even know I was alive," she said offhandedly, praying her very real hurt didn't show.

But it showed as plainly as the murky dawn creeping over the skylight of the studio. Alex, who never considered himself perspicacious, realized at once the pain he must have caused Jane, who had been impressionable and inexperienced, and in all probability still was. He must remember that in the future.

"I had many things pressing on my mind at the time, and wasn't fit company for anyone," Alex said, hoping his answer would be sufficient.

"I realized something was amiss, but I was too self-centered to believe that I mattered less than any weighty problem you might have," she said tentatively. "Can you tell me what was troubling you."

Alex wanted to confide all the horror plaguing him in Ireland. However, he weighed the consequences of ruining his colonel's illustrious fifty years of service to England and tarnishing the man's fine reputation in the bargain and chose to keep quiet.

"Someday, Jane, I hope I can tell you the whole tragic story, but I see I have stayed far too long."

"I think you carry a heavy burden still."

Alex was drawn to Jane's degree of sympathy. It made him want to unburden himself then and there.

"I have never told anyone except Wellington," Alex said.

Jane waited.

He placed his teacup on a small table and heard himself talking about things he never thought he would tell anyone.

"In the heat of battle I accidentally unseated and wounded a young cavalry officer. When I went to help him I discovered he was a French army courier in disguise," Alex said, his hands shaking, his voice hoarse. "He was carrying a fortune in British money and a coded message. I am not proud to say I took advantage of his near-delirium to persuade him to tell me his mission. He finally told me it was payment for a high-ranking officer in my own regiment."

"How terrible for you."

"You can't imagine—no one can. Colonel Brinton was my brother's godfather, a friend of my parents, in and out of my life. It was he, above anything, that made me want to be a soldier, and here I was about to ruin his life," Alex said. "All because my horse stumbled over a wounded horse, throwing me across this boy's body, my saber piercing his chest."

Alex burrowed lower in the chair, his fingers plowing through his hair. "It was hell. Unmitigated hell. In one stroke I killed a young boy and was to destroy a man I loved like my father."

Jane remained silent. A wiser voice told her Alex would be appalled later by what he now revealed of himself. He would not thank her for causing him to break his silence. She did not know where the wisdom to hold back came from, but she heeded it.

"You might as well know the rest," Alex said, rising from his chair to circuit the studio again. "I kept the money and the message until after the battle. Then I asked Captain Tarn Maitland, a powerful man in the city, to investigate the colonel's finances. He told me that large sums of money had been in and out of his accounts at Coutts' Bank at times that corresponded suspiciously with the rise and fall of Napoleon's fortunes. Added to that was a record of financial profligacy that bordered on lunacy, almost as if the money burned a hole in his pocket, and he couldn't wait to be rid of it."

"Didn't you have him dead to rights with the coded message and the young soldier's confession?"

"I wasn't sure they were genuine, you see. I needed incontrovertible proof. I couldn't afford to be wrong, could I?" Alex came to stand beside her, his face a picture of grief. "I had to be satisfied that once I approached Wellington, I'd left no stone unturned."

Alex resumed his pacing.

"I went to Paris, and through my friend, Captain Gronow, met an old spy master for Napoleon, who confirmed that a high-ranking English officer had supplied the French with valuable information before and after Napoleon's exile. Interestingly, he never gave them the secrets of our regiment, only of the movements of others. Odd the way sentiment and loyalty work."

"What did Wellington say?"

"He was stunned, of course, for, like everyone else, he liked and respected Colonel Brinton. After what I told him, Wellington said it made a great deal of sense. Of those occasions when Napoleon seemed prepared for them, it was always after a meeting of his most trusted officers. He'd been suspicious, but until I set my findings before him, he never knew whom to blame."

"How could someone do such a horrid thing?" Jane asked. "Surely he could have raised money elsewhere?"

"He confessed to me that it wasn't just the money. He could have married for money," Alex said sadly, coming to sit next to Jane again. "Early in his career he had been accused of compromising a general's daughter in India. He was exonerated, but it was in his military records, and he never attained the rank of general he felt he deserved. God knows he was eminently qualified far more than many of his friends who reached the rank. He was going to pay back the army in the only way he knew—consorting with the enemy." Alex took up his cape and prepared to leave.

"And now I must go. I have said too much. I will regret this."

Jane rose with him and led the way to the door. She put her hand on his arm.

"What happened to your colonel?"

Alex shook uncontrollably. Would he never be free of the guilt that haunted his every waking moment?

"He shot himself in the tradition of disgraced officers. But first he cut off his tongue."

Chapter Twenty-two

It became almost a nightly ritual for Jane to expect Alex at the studio after his evening roamings about the town.

They never again alluded to the tragedy he had revealed to her. Studying her earlier sketches of Alex in Ireland and the ones she had painted since coming to London, it was clear to Jane that a subtle and important difference was to be found in the latest sketches. To her practiced eye, Alex appeared less taut, less grim around the eyes and mouth, and she wanted to believe the difference was his telling her of the guilt he still carried with him.

It was well past midnight, and Jane was impatient for Alex's arrival. She had a surprise for him.

At the point she was sure this would be one of those rare nights when he didn't appear and didn't send an explanation, Alex arrived looking magnificently heroic and handsome. A black evening coat with red satin lining floated behind him, and a shiny silk hat sat at a jaunty angle on his thick, curly hair. She wanted nothing more than to throw herself at him and have his arms enfold her. Hard as it was, she went on painting.

Alex made straight for the easel to study what Jane was working on. The sight set him back on his heels. It was halfway between a portrait and a large miniature, the kind she seemed to favor most, and he was the sitter! Clearly she had been working in secret. The face was finished, but, as always, the background—Waterloo on the dawn of battle—was only lightly suggested. It was the first time he had seen her use background in one of her pieces.

Alex studied the work from several angles, too moved to say anything. The man staring back at him was not the Alex he recognized anymore. This one had compassion and melancholy limned in gray eyes, a mouth untouched by the savagery and carnage of war, illusions undimmed. He wanted to be that man, and maybe one day in the lost past had been.

"You've idealized me, my dear Jane," he managed to say. "I could never be that man."

"You hate it. I can tell," Jane said, her arms tightly wound around her slim body, feeling every kind of fool for allowing Alex or anyone to see the work. She was mad to think she could capture this complicated man who had shadowed her life for so long. He was a man who made all other men pale in comparison. She, least of all, had the skill to show the Alexander Barrington so hidden from the world.

Alex moved toward her, wanting to console her for misinterpreting his words, wanting to hold her in his arms and thank her for portraying him as a man of ideals and character he would never dare claim for himself.

A chilling gulf opened between them, and he stepped back, concerned he would say all that was in his heart and spoil the easy friendship they'd established over recent weeks. Besides, these meetings would have to end. He had received a rambling letter from John Lear saying he expected to be back in London soon, after Alex left for the fishing party in Scotland.

"Of course, I don't hate the portrait," Alex protested good-naturedly, hoping he did a good job of restoring her faith in herself. He had long since recognized that

Jane's art was as important to her as his army career had once been to him. How lucky she was to have something that meant so much to her.

He went to look at himself once again. "You've made me far more interesting than I really am, and that is what troubles me. People know me for a depraved, cynical wretch. They will admire your art for making me look quite angelic."

Jane wasn't in the least mollified, but if Alex wanted her to feel pleased, then she would have to play along with the fiction. She supposed that was all part of the game anyone who had to paint for money must endure. She had better learn to take her lead from her subjects. Could she tell Alex the truth? *I painted you as I want you to be and believe you to be—vulnerable, brave, and utterly human. The love of my life.* But to hint the truth of her feelings for him would send him running for the hills, and that was something she wouldn't risk.

"Come now, you should be proud," Alex said, striding across the studio to stand beside her. She was vigorously cleaning her brushes. Whatever happened, he would always remember Jane busy with her brushes, her lower lip caught between her teeth in characteristic concentration, her lustrous blue-black hair escaping her chignon, her clothes stiff with paint. She was the least vain woman he had ever met, and more and more alluring.

Alex shook himself. She was his best friend's fiancée, and he had no right to let his mind wander down dangerous byways.

"My mother will love the portrait. This is the way she chooses to see me." He laughed.

"I can assure you she will make a great display of it. You will be inundated with commissions by people with bad characters, who will expect you to make them better than they are."

Jane turned on him. "Is that what you think I am, a fawner, a flatterer?" She threw the brushes aside, stalking away from him.

"Of course I don't think you would be dishonest. Far from it," he said forlornly, wishing he had put a bridle on his tongue. "The fact is, I am deeply embarrassed by your seeing me as you did, without my warts and wens. I am flattered beyond words, and I said those stupid things to cover my confusion."

Jane turned back and looked at him long and hard, certain that her love did not imagine his goodness, hidden by a robe of disinterest and self-indulgence he wore for the world to see. What he must have been before Waterloo and his colonel's crimes. No wonder Patrick adored him, John Lear worshipped him, and Uncle James admired him. They knew Alex for what he was.

Jane returned to the easel.

"I hope you are telling me the truth," she said. "I could easily destroy it."

Without knowing he was going to do it, Alex moved toward her, meaning only to give her an affectionate hug. All he wanted to do was reassure her. Jane was taken by surprise, unable to believe she was actually in Alex's arms. She knew she should pull away, pretend to be offended, but the fulfillment of the yearnings of days and nights were more than flesh could endure. She couldn't deny or fight against the only chance she would ever have to be so close to him.

Alex knew he was making a great mistake, indeed was behaving like a fool. He was mesmerized by the feel of Jane's long, slender body against him. He held back, kissing her far more lightly and casually than he wanted, her lips tantalizing him with their fullness and inexperience. The smell of her was like flowers rampant in a field; the softness of her hair under his fingers, the finest silk.

Alex pulled back from the brink of what he knew could be the biggest mistake of his life. To harm Jane and John Lear by injudicious lust would be to put himself beyond the pale. He must learn to keep himself in bounds, or risk the censure of every decent man and woman. He needed to make amends at once. Rarely in the years of his exile had he heeded the wiser part of his nature, but this time there was no other way. How he envied John Lear. What an adventure it would be to open such a woman to the exquisite pleasures of love. Even the fleeting seconds holding Jane told him that in the hands of a kind and experienced lover, she would respond like a flower to sun.

Alex shook off the enticing picture his head was making for him and turned to defuse as much as he could of the lapse they had shared.

"I always kiss ladies who make me seem nicer than I am," he said airily, when he was certain he could master the beating of his heart. "I predict a great career as a portraitist, my dear Jane."

Jane sensed volcanic changes in Alex, even if she didn't understand them. Of course he regretted his actions. And why not? Any man would be disgusted with her unseemly eagerness, her easy response. What a fool she was, throwing herself into the arms of a jaded man-about-the-*ton*, who had half the women of London panting after him.

"I shall hold you to your prediction. And when honest sitters tell me what a bad likeness I have painted, I shall send them to you to change their minds," she said at last.

By God, I have learned two great lessons tonight, Jane thought, fighting down a swelling river of tears: *In London, when a paragon kisses a woman, it means nothing, even if it means all the world to her; and I can lie and cheat with the best of them. A very instructive evening, one that will go a long way toward making me a success.* Jane braced her shoulders and looked boldly at Alex. After all, she was a Daitry of Ireland, wasn't she?

Alex chose to believe the kiss meant nothing to her, while he still trembled inside. He was disappointed, and grateful, too. But not too grateful. Maybe he was a better actor than he knew.

He could see that Jane was worn to cinders, and prepared to leave.

"Tomorrow I shall send my valet Atkins for the painting. I plan to present it to my mother at teatime. I shall report her reaction tomorrow night after my regimental dinner."

Jane agreed, and led him to the door, where the guard sat slumbering in a chair.

"He has better sense than we do," Alex remarked. Then he saluted and was gone.

Jane picked up a small branch of candles and blew out the rest before taking a last look at the portrait.

She felt impelled to run her fingertips over Alex's lips. But then she stepped back. They seemed to come alive under her touch. *What am I doing? What's happening to me?*

Chapter Twenty-three

Alex rose heavily to his feet to join in a toast to yet another hero and yet another battle in which the regiment had given valiant account of itself. He suppressed a yawn, which only exacerbated his headache.

For the first time since he was a green subaltern fresh out of Sandhurst, Alex wanted to be anywhere but at a regimental dinner. Once a highlight of his life, the noise, the smoke, the sight of men with the courage of lions slumped over the tables, their heads among the litter of dinner, made him anxious to be gone to the one place that increasingly drew him.

He looked at his watch. It was close to one o'clock. He pushed back his chair and pretended to weave out of the room. Fortunately, in the condition of his former comrades-in-arms, his departure would be of little moment.

Alex left the mess and welcomed the cool night air ruffling his hair. He lit a cheroot and walked double-time toward Jane's studio, the thought of a few hours in her company loosening the tightness in his temples. He had wonderful news for Jane. His mother was ecstatic about the portrait and had ordered it hung over the fireplace in the morning room. He was sure Jane would love knowing her work replaced a prized Holbein portrait of an ancestor. He couldn't wait to tell her.

The day had been extraordinary. With only a few hours of sleep, and those fitful, he was energized as he hadn't been for years. He'd breakfasted and been at his desk without food or drink until five. During the sleepless night it had come to him that his friends were dragging their feet on many of the schemes he had proposed for his starving men and their families. Disgusted with the small progress being made, Alex had set in train a whole new plan of jobs and apprenticeships for twenty-five of the most needy of his charges. It would cut into his income for the next year, but he felt better than he had in months.

Maybe he would become the idealized man Jane painted. He quickened his step, and was knocking on the gate at the back of the garden even sooner than he expected. The watchman was quick to let him in, and, whistling, Alex made for the studio.

Instead of Jane, he was astonished to find James Manley waiting for him. He stopped in his tracks. Was something wrong?

"I see my presence is a shock to you," the old man said, his eyes merry behind thick glasses.

"Rather," Alex said uneasily. Did this mean the old codger knew of his meetings with Jane? Did he disapprove, and was this to be the end of what had become to Alex the most important hours of the day? With the exception of the Legion, he had little in his life of great moment.

"Don't fret, Barrington," Manley said cheerfully. "I know and approve of your meetings with Jane. You have given her a great deal more address than she had when she first came here. And I saw your portrait. She has improved greatly, hasn't she?"

"Yes, she has. Where is Lady Jane?" Alex asked, emboldened by Manley's approval. "She usually tells me when she will be away."

"I persuaded her to accompany my sister to the opera and afterward to the Fieldings' supper party,"

Manley said smoothly. "They will be home soon, but I wanted a chance to talk to you before they returned."

Alex nodded and took the chair the old man pointed to on his left. He offered Alex a cheroot and a balloon glass already half filled with a tawny-colored liquid.

"You may very well tell me to mind my own business, and in your shoes I would probably have done just that, but I hope you will hear me out."

Alex lifted the glass and drank, not nearly as calm as he hoped he appeared. Lord James Manley was a deep one.

"Do you think John Lear is right for our Jane?" Lord James asked casually.

Alex didn't know where to turn or what to say. If Manley had asked him a few weeks earlier, before he and Jane had had their long, lovely meetings, his answer would have been an emphatic yes. But now Alex wasn't sure of anything.

"John Lear is a fine man, sir, and he will do all in his power to make Lady Jane happy." The truth hurt Alex as never before. But would Jane be happy with Lear? Suddenly the collar of his uniform was choking him. His stomach was aflutter, and he couldn't seem to get a proper grip on himself.

"You can't think of anyone else who might suit Jane more, can you?" the old man asked, studying Alex, quite aware that his young friend was extremely uncomfortable, and his normally tanned complexion decidedly pale.

"I can't imagine anyone who would suit Jane better," Alex insisted, trying to convince himself that what he was saying was true.

"I am so glad we had this talk, Barrington," the old man said, rising ponderously from his chair, his suspicions confirmed. But it gave him no peace, in fact it made him terribly heartsick. "Naturally, my sister and

I do not know Mr. Lear as well as you do. I rely on your endorsement."

"You can indeed."

"And you, Alex, do you not plan to marry and set up your own nursery?"

"Not a hope, my lord," Alex laughed.

"Take my advice, dear boy." James Manley looked long and stern at his young friend. "I once thought as you, and now I'd give anything if Jane were my daughter. Life is barren indeed when all you have are yearnings for what might have been. The pursuit after every well-turned ankle, perfect oval face, and eyes like velvet ends one day, as it must, and what you have then are long, empty nights. I don't recommend it."

Alex felt a sudden senseless chill down his spine, or was someone walking over his grave? He didn't know.

"Loneliness is hell, Alex," he said, examining his well-kept hands. "Worse is knowing you have no flesh and blood to carry you along down the years. Perpetuating oneself is a law of nature and becomes a sense of terrible loss when it is too late." Manley shrugged. He could only talk from his experience. If only he were forty years younger!

"I'll send Jane to you when she returns."

Alex nodded and reached for the decanter. He'd heard all Manley's arguments before from his mother. And his brother Edward was a ranking bore on the subject of his children and his pride in keeping the Barrington line well supplied. If they couldn't reach him, Manley had even less hope of success. He was too selfish, liked his own way too much. He needed solitude as few men did. Damn, damn, damn.

The silly lapse when Manley first asked him about John Lear as a husband for Jane was just that, a momentary lapse. Alex rose quickly, almost knocking over the small table. He looked at the carriage clock Jane kept near her easel. A half hour had gone by since the old man left. As he turned to take up his cape and hat, Jane came into the studio.

She was flushed, her smart mauve silk evening dress cut low at the neck showed her bosom at its best, her eyes indeed velvet. For once her onyx hair was in place, each strand constrained. Alex missed the wayward wisps, and he itched to free her hair. Jane was beautiful, lithe, moving with a new grace to her step. Where was the woman who drew him to the studio every night?

"Uncle James told me you were here," she said, breathless, an amused look in her eyes. "Of course, Aunt Madge was out of earshot. She would never approve of you here at this hour."

"Yes, I know. I am curious. How long has James known that I come here?" Alex asked.

"I suspect he knew from the beginning. He watches over me like a mother hen." She laughed.

"You are very fortunate."

Jane nodded. "He worries about me as no one ever has," she said, thinking of her own father, remote and disagreeable so often during her childhood.

"He is not overbearing?"

"Hardly. You, of course, as the heir of a large family, must have been overloved."

Alex never thought about it, and now that she forced him to consider it, remembered how much he had indeed been doted upon. "I found it cloying actually. When I went into the army, I thought my father would have a stroke."

"How different our experiences were," Jane said, surprised she could talk this way. It was too late to repine over her parents, but the wreck of their marriage was something she would never repeat. When John Lear returned, she would make her feelings perfectly clear. Her heart was given freely to the man standing so majestically across the room in his glorious Guards' uniform, with the row of medals gleaming in the candlelight. How her fingers hungered to touch him.

Alex thought Jane had forgotten he was in the room. He felt certain their talk about their childhood accounted for the quiet that descended on the studio. Had her childhood been so different from his? She should have been cosseted like his sister and her friends, but an instinct he trusted told him Jane would not like him to probe. He had good news for her, and he was going to tell her at once. Anything to wipe away the strain he saw on her face.

"My mother was overjoyed with the painting, and is anxious to meet you and pose for you when she gets back from my nephew's baptism." He watched Jane's reaction, and it was all he could hope.

"She wants to sit for me?" At once Jane's eyes sparkled. "A woman who sat for Gainsborough? I don't believe it."

"She is looking forward to meeting the artist who saw things in her 'dearest son' that no one else has," he mimicked mockingly.

What she and I see, my darling Alex, is what you could be and are through the eyes of the women who love you. Jane wanted to say the words aloud, but never would. Instead she sat down heavily in a chair, still reeling from the news that the Dowager Countess of Trent wanted to sit for her.

"I have a terrible feeling I shall disappoint her," Jane murmured when she could trust her voice. She was afraid of giving herself away to Alex's mother. Surely she had seen in her portrait all the things Jane didn't want anyone to suspect. From the first, Alex's portrait was a labor of love, and she had been aware when she was painting that her touch had never been more sure, possibly even inspired. The portrait was finished almost too quickly, yet she didn't change a stroke. A strange force, something unique, seemed to guide her hand and give her the confidence she lacked in the finished pictures of Aunt Madge and Uncle James.

"You are very quiet." Alex longed to take her in his arms and wipe away the worry lines around her mouth. It was a wish that came much too often for his peace of mind and when he least expected it. Clea was becoming suspicious, hinting ever so subtly that he wasn't making love to her because he had found someone prettier and younger. What else could he do but deny it vehemently, perhaps trying to convince himself more than Clea.

Alex shook his head. These wild musings would get him and Jane in trouble, and he couldn't bear hurting anyone so innocent.

"Really, Jane," Alex said, reaching for her hand, almost unaware he was doing it. "I am sure most artists, writers, and poets have moments of doubt about their abilities, but they soldier on, surely?"

How often she wanted to feel those steel-like, tapered fingers entwined in hers, wanted them—if the truth were told—all over her in those nocturnal fantasies she only dimly understood.

Alex was stunned by his action. Of course she would disengage her hand. Someone with Jane's sensibilities would naturally be offended by such familiarity. After all, she was promised to another man, and such intimacy could never be countenanced. Before he could find the words to apologize for his lapse, Jane went on to other matters, and he was pleased and grateful for her exquisite tact. She could very easily have taken offense—most women would have—and then where would he be? It was much easier to talk about painting, and she took up the thread of their conversation.

"I have been completely isolated from other artists, but not of my own choosing," Jane said. She was determined to put a safe distance between them, and retreated to the safety of her easel and brushes.

Alex went to study a part of the studio where many pictures were haphazardly stacked.

"What an unusual collection you have," Alex observed. "Such vivid faces of English men and women."

"Irish, too."

"I stand corrected. I see you do the faces and surround them with much white space. Are they preliminary to full portraits?"

"No. I like faces unadorned. They are character studies of people who interest me. I think too much background often dilutes the person—good, evil, or nonentity."

Alex stepped closer. She spoke low in a faraway voice, as if talking to herself. He was enthralled.

"To me at least, one cannot mask so easily the real person in a miniature. I do not want to enhance personality by diaphanous dresses and luxurious clothes or lush landscapes," she said, putting down her brushes and warming to her arguments. "Charming children at their parents' knees, elegant dogs, and purebred horses are important and lovely, to be sure, but they do not tell me anything about the parents, except they are usually attractive, fertile, and can afford expensive animals and large estates."

"I had no idea you were such a moralist."

"I suppose I am," she said, returning to work. " I hadn't thought so. I prefer to say I like truth, and I think it is incumbent on artists to be honest."

"You are a dreamer, Jane. We all have something to hide."

"My terrible handicap is that I know little of the world, and may not recognize good and evil very well. It will come one day, I hope," she concluded.

"Should many patrons like to be seen so naked before the world? Aren't you asking too much of human nature? I don't imagine many people want the truth of a less-than-godlike-character set down for their contemporaries and descendants to see.

"How fortunate you are, Jane, to be able to indulge your principles. It is not always given to people to be honest and honored for honesty."

Jane looked up, realizing that he was referring to the cloud under which he had left the army. They never referred to the night he had told her about Colonel Brinton.

"I am especially taken with these," Alex said, pausing at another stack of rough studies lying in a corner.

Jane came quickly to take them away. What if he had found a sketch of himself, any one of the dozens she had hidden away from prying eyes? She held the drawings close to her breast.

"A secret hoard, are they?"

"In a way. I have been experimenting with a new form for myself."

"Tell me. I love a secret," he said, leaning against the old greenhouse wall, his long legs encased in black, skin-tight trews, crossed at the ankles. He was a picture of masterful self-confidence.

Jane didn't know quite what to do. He was so charming, so seemingly interested that her reserve, so carefully husbanded all her life, began to thaw a little.

"Do you know about the blocks of unfinished Michelangelo marbles in Florence called 'The Slaves'?"

"I went into the army and missed having the Grand Tour, and have never seen them. But isn't there some mystery about them?"

"I don't know a great deal. I have seen only amateur renderings and been told various secondhand stories by visitors who have been to Italy. As I understand it, when he began to work on the blocks, he felt he was uncovering bodies buried in the marble, who were begging him to release them from their bondage."

Alex reached out, and Jane gave him several of the studies. He looked through them.

"How exciting. Indeed, your subjects seem to emerge from the canvas."

"You do see what I am trying to do!"

"I do. You are wrong to hide bold experimentation. Isn't that what makes the difference between painters . . . of originality and vision?" he asked. "I know little about art, but I know what thrills me."

"You are very kind," Jane said, walking back to the easel, touched by his interest, but puzzled, too. "I don't often discuss my work. I hope you are not patronizing me as so many do."

"On the contrary, I am flattered that you would explain your views to me." Alex felt he had made progress toward understanding this mercurial woman. But he was also aware of the momentary prickly note in Jane's voice, and knew he must tread carefully. He did not want to wear out his welcome. He went in search of his cap.

"I am a brute to keep you so late with my insistent curiosity about your work. You must be exhausted," he said, reaching to kiss Jane's hand. "Manley will bar the door to me surely for keeping you so late. I am afraid to think what Mrs. Brooks would say."

Jane was anything but tired and wanted to protest, but decided against it. She knew people had little patience for long discussions about art.

"May I call upon you again and resume where we left off?" Alex asked as she walked beside him toward the door. "I am occupied with my Legion tomorrow, but the day after I am promised to the Carterets' for a charity ball. I will come as early as I can."

Jane smiled. Perhaps, after all, she hadn't bored him to tears.

Chapter Twenty-four

Even the Junoesque figure and velvet voice of the magnificent Sarah Siddons in excerpts from her most famous Shakespearean roles failed to cool Alex's impatience to be with Jane.

Normally the most ardent admirer of the great actress before her retirement, he felt trapped and tried to think of a hundred excuses to leave the theater without insulting his hosts. When at last Mrs. Siddons made a long and theatrical bow to the audience, Alex slipped out of the Carterets' box at Drury Lane with mumbled excuses about a sick headache.

After a mad dash in a hired hack, Alex arrived at the studio an hour earlier than he expected, and found Jane completely absorbed and oblivious to his arrival.

"Who are you painting now?" he asked, stealing up beside her. "A new work so soon, and so advanced."

Jane turned, a scant smile acknowledging his presence, and turned back to her easel at once. It would not do to show her wild happiness. It wouldn't do for the Earl of Trent to suspect how much his visits meant to her. It wouldn't do at all.

"He is Matthew Piroschap, the young son of a family who was especially kind to me when I traveled to London with Aunt Madge," she said easily. "I did several sketches of the boy while I was a guest in his parents' home. I tore up most that were not right, but I saved several to remember what he looked like."

"It looks like a large miniature," Alex noted.

"How observant you are," Jane said, her blue eyes alive once again. Alex was so unlike John, who never inquired or showed the least interest in her work other than fleeting and polite inquiries.

"Why do you want to paint miniatures above all else, when you are so clearly a fine and original portrait painter? You would be much more honored."

"It appears to be in my nature to make things difficult for myself" Jane said sheepishly. In fact, she was unwilling to be completely honest with Alex or anyone about all the real reasons miniatures loomed so large in her life. "The fact is, miniatures are very romantic. They have long been used in the highest circles of statecraft."

"Romantic?"

"If a political marriage was contemplated, a court miniaturist would make special renderings for ambassadors to bring to the other *parti*. Isn't that romantic enough, even for you?"

"I hadn't thought about it, frankly. You remind me now that Mama had my batman pack some of the family miniatures in my field desk when I was a young officer." Alex said. "The one of my father was very consoling when he died and I could not return to England for his funeral."

"I painted some of Patrick when he was home from Eton and Sandhurst. Very simple, but they always kept him close to me," Jane said. "Miniatures have a place in the world. You cannot imagine how much. The only trouble is that the few superb ones I have seen by Nicholas Hilliard and Isaac Oliver make me want to hide my head in shame. I will never attain their excellence."

Alex noted her wistfulness. He sensed she would only tell him as much as she wanted him to know. What she did not say was as fascinating as what she did say. He had never found the same mystery in other women who had interested him through the years.

"Sometimes I wish I didn't want the impossible," Jane said, more to herself than Alex, "but when I have enough money, I am going to study with Claude Morgan, if he'll have me. Then I shall have put myself to the touch."

"If it's a matter of money . . . .?"

"Not you, too. Aunt Madge and Uncle James have overwhelmed me with kindness. I cannot keep taking charity. I can't. It quite makes me wild."

He should have known better. He wasn't in the least surprised by her vehemence. He wanted her to have everything his considerable fortune could buy. He wanted to make her happy, but her future husband had that for the giving. He frequently, too frequently, forgot John Lear. It wouldn't do to continue in that folly.

The very idea sent chills down his back.

"You know, of course, many artists, Martin Archer Shee especially, are most unkind about miniaturists. He suggests they are lazy and only artists for the money," Alex commented.

"No. I did not know his feelings. How terrible. He may be a fine artist, but I doubt his character. To be so unkind to others whose visions differ from his is disgraceful. And the thought that Richard and Mary Cosway, Andrew Robertson, and Emma Kendrick are beneath his touch is monstrous."

Her anger flared, and she strode about the room like a tigress.

Alex was thrilled. He knew Jane had spirit, but he had never seen her so on fire. Her eyes darkened, her hands tightened into fists. What a far cry from the lost and lonely woman he had first met in Ireland, in what now seemed centuries ago.

"How curious you never mentioned Shee's libel before this," she said, peering at him closely.

"I was meaning to tell you that I met him a few

weeks ago," he started to say. "No, I must be honest. Because of you, I asked my neighbor in Portland Square, Richard Rush, the American minister to London, to allow me to accompany him to the anniversary dinner of the Royal Academy of Arts at Somerset House."

"Were any of the women members of the RA present?"

"None, I am afraid."

"I will never understand. Whoever decides these things allowed us to be among the founders of the Academy. They deign to exhibit our work at the annual exhibitions, but we are not welcome to teach or attend their great, famous dinner meetings. You and your American are welcomed, but not a woman painter. It makes my Irish blood boil," she fumed. "Surely men and women have the same aspirations and talent. Is it a crime to be a woman?"

"No. But it isn't often I have the chance to observe a woman tilting at government and public windmills, a subject very close to my heart at the moment," he said. "I know about official indifference, my dear, and it hurts to whistle in a wilderness, doesn't it?"

"I am not often pleased with your fellow men." Jane grinned. "But tell me your own views of women in art, music, and letters. No lies, please. I shall know."

"You must meet my mother." Alex chuckled. "As children, we grew up combing *artistes* out of our hair. Mama befriends anyone who comes to her and has what she calls 'gifts.'"

"That's the most evasive answer I ever heard," Jane said. "Why do I waste my time?"

"Surely you know I have never belittled your devotion." He didn't like explaining himself. "Perhaps I shade my answer. Maybe I was not as thoughtful as I should have been. But I hope I have never been intolerant, never rude to her earnest friends, the ones who work at their crafts. It's the ones who would have liked to have painted the great picture, composed the great symphony, and written the latest important book who irritate me. They talk well, but do nothing."

"And I am not playing at being an artist?"

Alex looked around the studio and lifted his eyebrows.

"Hardly."

"I only wish Patrick and others understood the difference as you seem to."

And why should she be surprised that Alex, more than most people she knew, gave her high marks for working so hard. To everyone else she was an oddity, and she stopped asking for more. She thought of Aunt Madge and her brother, and John Lear, and sighed. Despite their words, it seemed as if they merely tolerated her foibles.

"I have tired you. Shall I go?" Alex asked in a gentle voice.

No, my dear Alex, she wanted to say, *I don't want you to go. I never want you to leave. Can't you tell? Can't you feel it?*

"I am glad of the company. Friends of artists must be encouraged," she said, eager for more time with him. "Besides, I am now a professional, and must encourage patronage."

"That's a far cry from the way you once felt about anyone watching you, especially me," he reminded her. "Now will you sell me that nice young man you're working on?"

"Are you feeling sorry for me?"

"What a terrible thing to say. If you knew me better, you would know I never do things out of pity."

"Nonsense. Your purse is open to all those soldiers and seamen of yours. Don't deny it. Mr. Lear tells me everything," she said, smiling at him. "I meant to congratulate you on your efforts. I see the poor souls and their pitiful families everywhere, dragging themselves and their wounds, shuffling along with their empty sleeves and makeshift sticks, looking so abandoned, so hopeless. What upsets me most are the quality, who push them aside like dirt under their boots."

"I would not like to tell you the names of my richest acquaintances, who never spent a moment in the war, and who refuse to join us in finding ways to help them. They blame the lot of the men and their families on what they choose to call 'their sloth.' "

"You must be proud of yourself."

"You congratulate me for nothing. The work my friends and I support is a mere pittance. More will come to London for relief every day. The navy was one hundred thousand strong in 1815, and thirty-five thousand the next year. With the end of the war there is less need for our goods on the Continent. Our agriculture is in a deplorable state," he said, his face grave. "Have you heard about the blanketeers?"

"Who?"

"They carry their blankets and possessions everywhere. They have no homes and are on the march in the eastern counties. Our efforts are only a ripple in a sea of misery. The government should be responsible for these men. They seduced them into war with every wile they knew, and then abandoned them without a parting kiss."

Alex smiled warily at Jane, concerned that his language might not suit the ears of a maiden lady. Alex was grim when he said, "A bit dramatic, but that's the way it is."

Jane put down her paint brush and covered the small canvas.

"If Patrick is having a bad time of it with Daitry Hall, no money or a strong man to work alongside his tenants, what can these people expect?"

"Ah yes, I forgot." Alex said. Let us talk again about

the picture you are working on. May I have it? I will treasure it."

"You must assure me you are not buying this out of pity for me."

"I may not know a great deal about art, but I do know what I like. Every painting I buy strikes a chord in me, and I must want to live with it." *In this case*, he thought, *I want the artist* and *the painting*.

"Then you shall have it."

"At a fair price. I insist on that."

Jane blushed. She hadn't the least idea how much to ask. She would have to seek out Uncle James for advice.

"And one day, Jane, I want to talk to you further on this obsession of yours, if you will permit me to call it that."

"I never thought of what drives me as an obsession, but I see, my lord, that is precisely what I am. Obsessed. I know I disturb many, because I tend to erase every other consideration when I work. Thank you, my lord, for pointing this out to me. I will not change, however."

"Please. It is time to call me Alex."

"Alex." She laughed, the name tripping lightly off her tongue.

Alex nodded, remembering how bored he was when his mother's artist friends tried to discuss their work at great length with him. What a fool he'd been. He missed a whole world of experience. He wouldn't make the same mistake again.

"By the by, do you ride?"

"Do I ride? How dare you ask an Irishwoman that question. It's an impertinence. Riding is one of the best things I do."

Alex made her a bow. "Indeed, I regretted the question before it left my tongue. Then you must send me a note telling me when you can join me in the park tomorrow."

With that he saluted, and went into the night.

Chapter Twenty-five

The great white stallion tried to unseat the rider, and would have, except Alex—for whom a saddle was as natural as a drawing-room sofa—had him on a tight rein. He smiled, patted the animal's shiny coat, and gentled his ears.

The brute's impatience was nothing compared to his master's. Jane had promised to meet him at ten in a grove of trees on the east side of the park, and it was five minutes after the hour.

At the point where he began to worry, his eyes fastened on a magnificent bay just entering the park. He had very nearly bought a bay very much like it at Tattersall's two weeks before, but he had enough frisky horses in his stable. Now he regretted his decision. Whoever was riding knew how to handle the brute. On closer scrutiny, Alex was delighted to see Jane. She was not given to idle boasting. She rode magnificently.

Horse and rider came toward him at last at an elegant pace, and Alex was taken aback by the stunning picture she made in a magnificent superfine black-and-white riding costume with a small feathered hat, her chignon quite tame for a change. She grinned at him. He was surprised to feel a catch or something equally strange in his chest.

"I couldn't resist showing off Lightning," she said, coming up to him a little breathless. "I have never ridden a more wonderful horse."

"James Manley does know horseflesh," Alex said, chagrined that it was the old man, and not he, who had contributed so much to pleasuring Jane. With the studio and Manley's obvious affection for her, Jane was far from the graceless, melancholic country girl he had first met. She was an elegant beauty.

"Am I terribly late?" Jane asked, admiring the way he sat his horse, the perfect fit of his gray jacket over wide shoulders, and a foamy white stock with a heavy gold horseshoe pin in the center. She longed to paint him just as he was that morning. Why was today any different from most days? She chuckled to herself. Some of the poses she had in mind were not at all seemly for a maiden lady.

"Do let's exercise these great beasts and make everyone jealous," Jane said, leading the way, her groom at a safe distance behind. "Sometimes I can't decide what I love most, horses or painting."

"I think painting," Alex offered, catching up with her.

"My obsession." She laughed. "I like that. It justifies my inability to stop painting, even if I wanted to."

"I notice you are cast down one moment and exultant the next. I suppose it has to do with the progress you are making. Is there no middle course?"

"None. All I know is I am completely alive when I am painting. The day I can call myself an accomplished miniaturist and portrait painter, I shall ask for no greater happiness."

Alex thought she had never looked so young and carefree, even as part of him noted with regret that she seemed to leave no room for love or marriage.

"I am fascinated. Tell me why you must paint."

Jane looked at Alex unbelieving. For years she had longed to talk about her visions but had kept silent, knowing people would laugh, if they listened to her at all.

"When all goes well, I am blessed, I could climb mountains, slay dragons. But when what I see in my mind's eye becomes distorted on the canvas, I am crushed."

She stopped and looked helplessly at Alex. "Does this sound preposterous?"

He shook his head.

"I hate a white canvas. I am in terror of it. There is something hidden there and only I can make it come alive. When I fail, when I can't make my picture breathe, I feel an utter failure and I want to go away and hide. But when what I see and feel comes into being as I see it, I am worthwhile again, reborn."

"How marvelous."

"Sometimes, Alex, I think I would sell my soul to be a great artist."

"I envy you feeling so deeply about something. It must be glorious, and painful, of course."

"You do see?" Jane's heart sang. How wonderful! Alex did understand the demons driving her and all she had hidden from the world like an unpardonable sin.

Suddenly dirt and stones kicked up behind them. Jane turned. There, within a few feet, was the most startlingly beautiful woman Jane had ever seen.

"My lord, you must make me known to your companion," the woman said.

"Lady Clea Wesley, may I present Lady Jane Daitry," Alex obliged. "Lady Jane is an artist. She has just completed a portrait of me for my mother."

"Splendid, Lady Jane. I would like to sit for you," Clea said easily. "My husband wishes a new likeness of me for his rooms in Whitehall, and I have been searching wildly for an artist who would please me."

Alex had been afraid this would happen. He had lied and evaded all her questions about where he spent his nights. Would she be a proper influence on someone as impressionable as Jane? Could he deny Jane the chance to make the money she wanted so desperately? Clea had a great deal of influence in London, and many women slavishly followed her like lapdogs.

"My lady, I am not as accomplished as I would like to be," Jane protested.

Alex felt Jane's hesitation. Their talk had made him more understanding of her fears, and he felt protective. It was a very new experience for him. It was time to change the subject and give Jane a moment to make up her mind. Besides, he wanted to end the meeting as soon as possible. Madge Brooks would not be well pleased to know Jane had made the acquaintance of his mistress, no matter how accidental the meeting.

"Lady Jane would like to study miniatures with someone like Claude Morgan. Could you tell her about him?" Alex asked, urging his horse forward. He didn't want to divert traffic or attract too much attention to them from the few riders abroad at that hour.

"Some say Claude was on his way to becoming the equal of Robertson and Cosway, but he was eccentric and importunate. He pressed Lady Bennem for payment of several much-admired miniatures he made of her, and she cut him dead."

"How dare he be paid for his labors?" Alex responded. "The old dragon owes the world and its brother."

"Darling, I haven't paid my dressmaker for a year," Clea trilled airily. "She knows I will get to her bills one day. After all, I bring her all my friends. And now that my daughter is to be married to the heir of a dukedom, she should pay me."

Jane understood that Clea Wesley intended to relegate her to status of her dressmaker, and she wouldn't have it. There was no way she would consent to paint the jade. No possibility at all.

"And now, my dears, I must be off." Clea wheeled her horse and was away.

"What an extraordinary woman," Jane said, watching Clea and her groom gallop toward Tattersall's end of Hyde Park.

"People have called her worse than that," Alex replied.

"Tell me about her." Jane was intrigued. She had little personal experience of highborn English ladies, and after meeting Clea Wesley, she wasn't sure she wanted to, much less paint anyone so patronizing.

"Clea can bring about a great difference in your career," Alex said. "She can make an artist or writer, if it suits her. The *ton* follow her dictates in the arts, if nothing else."

She might not want such a patroness, one so obviously negligent about money and the feelings of others, but could she refuse to listen? *Would she treat me the way she treats her modiste? Do I have the right to be too nice in my choice of assistance, when Patrick writes each week of his difficulties?* Her head hurt with arguments. It was useless to be proud or particular.

Alex and Jane rode in silence. Clea had spoiled the wonderful day for them. At the exit nearest the Manley House, Alex made the announcement that once would have given her immense joy.

"I leave for Scotland tomorrow on my yearly holiday at Lord Burner's place," he said, before he left her. He was looking for a sign that she would miss their late-night talks as much as he. If he had hoped to see anything beside mild surprise at his departure, he was badly disappointed.

"John begged off this year," Alex said, not in the least pleased to see Jane blush at the mention of Lear's name.

"I had a letter from Mr. Lear this morning. He arrives at the end of the week. He will not be pleased to miss you."

Alex nodded, struck by the way she called John "mister," even now, when they were about to publish the banns. Other women might be hidebound in such matters of propriety, but it seemed strange on the lips of Jane Daitry. She seemed to set little store by conventions. But what was he doing looking for signs of indifference? Scotland would cure him. Good sport and friends of years was all that he needed to be himself again.

Jane took Alex's distracted look to mean he couldn't think of anything more to say. She would help him and end the uncomfortable silence. It was time she started to live without their meetings, the sound of his step, the sight of him filling the doorway and lighting the studio as no world of candles would ever do. She would not have him to herself. And why did she expect more? To him she was Patrick's sister, and nothing more.

"I will miss our talks," Alex said, kissing her hand. "They have been so instructive."

Alex could have not said anything more calculated to shatter her. *What a fool I am. There could never be anything more between us than his kind concern for my ambitions.* Jane bade her groom to follow, setting her horse to a canter, afraid Alex would see the tears flooding her eyes.

Chapter Twenty-six

Madge was back to disapproving of Alex Barrington.

"I was right from the first. Nothing but scandal will come of giving Alex Barrington the run of the house," Madge Brooks stormed at her brother. "I wouldn't be surprised if all my friends cut me dead. How could Jane do this to me? I quail at what John Lear will say."

"The girl couldn't know about Alex and Clea, could she?" For once, James Manley was on the point of agreeing with his sister. Alex Barrington was sometimes too ramshackle by half.

"More reason to bar Barrington from the house again. How could he subject our innocent girl to someone so notorious?"

"Who's notorious, Aunt Madge?" Jane came into the dining room.

"We understand you were introduced to Lady Clea Wesley in the park several days ago," Manley said carefully.

"She came up to us, and Lord Alex introduced her. She is a small Botticelli," Jane observed dryly.

Relieved, Manley scowled at his sister. If Alex had a *tendre* for Jane, he was certain he wouldn't hurt her.

"Really, Jane dear, you can't receive Mr. Lear looking like an Irish washerwoman," Madge said, quickly changing the subject.

"He will understand I have a lot of work to do." Jane finished her breakfast and rose from the table.

"Lady Clea will sit for me next week. Lord Alex is sure she will further my career, if she likes my painting." Jane winked at Manley.

"I won't allow it," Madge declared.

Jane came and knelt beside her benefactress. "Darling, I suspect Lady Clea is a bit notorious, but don't worry."

"James, do something."

Her brother shook his head.

"Do what you have to do, Jane, but remember you can have all you and your brother need from me. I am a very warm fellow, with more money than is good for me."

"I, too," Madge said.

"I know, and it is a great comfort to me. But you know us Daitrys. We have more pride than hair."

She rose from her knees and kissed Madge, then crossed to James to do the same.

Jane was having difficulties with the finishing touches needed on Matthew Piroschap's picture before she would allow Alex's servant to fetch it. It was a clear summer day, but still her fingers were numb and the roaring fire couldn't reach the cold within. She rubbed her hands and summoned her maid from the corner where she sat snoring, as usual.

"Lizzie, be a good girl and ask the butler for a small dram of Irish whiskey."

Lizzie encountered John Lear on her way out the door.

"What a nice little boy."

Jane put out her hand quickly. The thought that he might feel obliged to kiss her was too daunting.

"I was happy to hear your father is much improved," she said, all the other greetings she had rehearsed fading from her mind. She decided not to mince words. It was the only way to get the disagreeable job done quickly.

"John, I can't marry you. I like you more than I can say, but we wouldn't suit."

Lear looked as if he had been pole-axed. He sat down and his hat fell from his hands.

"You have always known how much my painting means, and it would take the most extraordinary man to be forever patient with me." Jane paused, her heart racing. "I can never be the kind of wife you deserve."

Lear looked around at the studio, taking side glances at Jane's faded and patched riding clothes, her long, black hair trailing over her shoulders. She was right, of course. An artist wife was not for him. He smiled and turned to take Jane's hand.

"I knew I was asking a great deal to expect you to love me," he said, his words measured, his smile kind, regretful. "I have waited a very long time to marry, and I have learned that what I want with all my heart is the life of a simple country squire. I am not a London fop, and never wanted to be. Alex will tell you that. I have traveled widely, but no place means more to me than England and my small village. I always knew that."

Delight and gratitude swamped Jane. He was releasing her without the least rancor.

"Thank you for not hating me."

"Hate you? I thank you with all my heart for making everything easy for me, dear Jane. I came here with a heavy heart. The terrible truth is, I found at home a dear lady, Miss Margaret Croft."

"It was terrible of me to send you away with the promise that I would marry you. You were so forlorn and so worried about your father, I couldn't bear to hurt you. I am so glad you have found someone to love."

Lear smiled shyly. "I will return home at once and

tell her of your generosity. You must meet sometime in the future."

Jane threw her arms around Lear's neck and kissed him on the cheek in a display of affection he had missed before. If only Jane had been loving, he would never have permitted himself to look on Margaret as anything more than a sweet and pretty friend to his sisters. Jane's kiss lingered on his cheek. He would always feel great affection for her, and a little part of him would always wonder what life would have been like with this remarkable woman. The only remaining problem would be telling Alex Barrington that the betrothal was off.

"It will take an extraordinary man to matter more to you than your painting," John said, grinning, though a frisson of regret lingered in his mind. "I love Margaret, but she will never be as intriguing as you, Jane Daitry."

Jane stepped back. A terrible thought came to her.

"Would you have married me if I hadn't cried off first?"

"Of course. I couldn't make you a laughingstock with your friends and Alex, and I was taken with you the moment we met."

"Poor John. You are the nicest young man and a dear idiot to offer for me when you didn't love me."

"I was enormously fond of you from the start, and all of Alex Barrington's machinations were quite unnecessary."

Jane's eyes narrowed.

"Your brother and Madge Brooks were determined to marry you off," he said, not sure he was right to say so. "Mrs. Brooks doesn't know, but your brother wrote and asked Alex to watch over you. I came to visit him the day he received the letter."

"And was he pleased when you fell in with his brilliant maneuvering? After all, you did exactly as he planned."

"One never knows with Alex, but I think he was very proud of himself. I suspected it was his intent all along to marry me off to you so his conscience could be eased. He isn't a bad fellow really, when you know him."

"I could argue that point with you, John," Jane said between gritted teeth. "I really could."

Chapter Twenty-seven

Madge Brooks was in hysterics. She stood up and knocked over her wineglass.

"I don't know who I am more furious with, that lily-livered John Lear, who could prefer a red-faced milk-maid, or Patrick for writing to Alex Barrington, when I expressly told him not to."

It was the culmination of the most painful dinner Jane had sat through since leaving Ireland. She rose to go to her room.

"Madge, there is no excuse for this Cheltenham drama," her brother said, waving a balloon glass half full of brandy at her back. "The thing is done, and no one hurt by it."

Manley winked at Jane. He was delighted. Lear might be the salt of the earth, a nice, mild-mannered gentleman to be sure. He never took a drink over the limit or smoked more than half a fine cigar, but he allowed the nearest voice—Madge's or Barrington's—to persuade him. He would never do.

His Jane needed a red-blooded man who could understand her passions, and Barrington was just the man. Unconventional, with a stout heart, Alex was a man who knew his own mind. Manley would bet anything that Alex would know how to gentle a spirited colt like Jane. But what the hell was the damn fool doing in Scotland when all this high drama was going on?

Jane pounded on the arm of her chair and brought an end to his musings.

"How kind of dear Alex Barrington to plan my life for me. How kind of Patrick and Aunt Madge, much as I love them, to think they could marry me off to any man in London," she said between clenched teeth. "Why would I lie when I say I don't want to marry at all? Why do they dismiss my wishes so cavalierly?" Jane barely stopped for her breath. "I will take every commission I can get, study with Claude Morgan, and go back to Ireland and set up as a traveling miniaturist doing work for anyone who will have me, at any price they will pay me."

Madge returned to the dining room a few minutes later.

"James, if you were the gentleman you call yourself, you would call John Lear out," Madge said, her anger not in the least abated. "Look at her. She's devastated."

"Aunt Madge, I've said this before. I have never felt anything but friendship for John Lear, and he is well rid of me."

Madge made to protest.

"No, it is true. With respect, darling, I would have made him a terrible wife, but he was pressured by you and Alex Barrington to offer for me. For that I blame Barrington more than you. As for Patrick, I shall blister the paper when I write to him."

"Patrick only meant it for your good."

"Yes, but why did he have to involve Barrington, when he knew I detested the man from the time he brought Patrick home to Ireland?"

"I have a headache, and this time I am going to bed," Madge announced suddenly. Summoning all her dignity, she left them alone in the library.

Manley was suddenly not sure about Alex as a prospective husband for Jane. He hadn't been aware they had known each other before they met in his morning room. It went a long way toward explaining Jane's rudeness to Barrington from the start. But surely all that was in the past. What he saw from his bedroom window looked suspiciously like a budding love to him. Perhaps Alex's attentiveness meant nothing more than politeness. He couldn't remember being so disappointed.

Jane rose to her feet.

"It pains me to tell you, but I must, Uncle James. I am going to welcome anyone to the studio who can pay me or further my ambitions. If some of those who come may not be to your liking, I will understand and paint them in their homes. Lady Clea Wesley is my first commission. Barrington tells me she can make or break an artist."

Manley took a long swallow of his drink.

"This is your home, and the studio is yours to do with as you wish," he said. "I will deal with Madge."

Jane kissed him, and left to resume working.

Manley watched Jane leave and refilled his glass. For an artist to be sponsored by the mistress of the wildest rake in London would make a feast for the London harpies.

Chapter Twenty-eight

Lady Clea Wesley studied the painter far more exhaustively than the painter studied the subject in the long hours she and Jane spent in the studio.

Jane was too pleased to care or even notice. Lady Clea was clearly all that Alex said, and more. She was not a dilettante, but a serious and discerning critic. Several suggestions helped make the portrait far better than it might have been.

"You are a natural artist, but it's a pity you never had good tuition," Clea said in her throaty, disdainful way. From anyone else, Jane might have resented the airy highhandedness. But Clea had style and taste, and Jane was coming to admire her.

"My dear, with my patronage and my knowledge, you will be a success," Clea was saying. "But why do you want to paint miniatures? They are so common, portable monstrosities, while portraits can grace the finest walls of the finest houses."

Clea looked around at the half-dozen women friends hanging on her every word. They were a new crop of bejeweled creatures dressed in the height of fashion. Clea invited them to the studio each day as if it were her own drawing room. They waited patiently until she wearied of posing and immediately fought for Jane to do preliminary sketches of them.

For the past three weeks, Jane had more work than she dreamed possible. If this continued, she could see her way to repaying Patrick and Verna, with enough left over to approach Claude Morgan. Tired to the bone, often seeing her patrons parading before her in the few hours she allowed herself to sleep, Jane felt sanguine about the future.

If a certain manly figure with piercing gray eyes intruded while she worked, she soon banished him to the back of her mind. Alex Barrington might be thanked for sending Lady Clea to her, but she wanted nothing more from him. He'd gone beyond anything Patrick might have asked of him. And if she remained unmarried, and she would, Alex could only blame himself. No man would ever do for her after those close and wonderful nights in the studio, when she had fooled herself into believing that Alex came because he was interested in her work and, hopefully, because he was a little fond of her.

"I say, Jane, you are far away. I want you to change some things in the portrait. I would not want anyone to be privy to what goes on behind my eyes, especially Alex Barrington."

"How odd, Clea. You always boast that Alex reads you like a book," one of Clea's admirers called out.

"What I said was Alex knows my body like a book," Clea threw off, looking pointedly at Jane. She had been waiting for the perfect moment to find out if this mouse was Alex's latest amour and the one keeping him out of her bed. Although it no longer mattered whether Jane was or not. For she'd done what she had set out to do—made Jane Daitry beholden to her. Her scheme was moving well along.

Comparing what she had to offer someone as passionate as Alex, and what this Irish nobody had, made her laugh. No accounting for taste. A stallion like Alex didn't stay in any pasture too long. Now that she had established that Jane loved Alex, she was well pleased.

"What a bad man Alex is. He told me about this poor, helpless, Irish painter who needed my assistance.

Remember that day in the park? It was all supposed to be an accidental meeting. How like him. He never tells one hand what the other is doing. Obviously, he neglected to tell you we have been such good friends for years."

Jane doubted Clea's elaborate story, and remained motionless, feeling a cold so penetrating it froze her heart. Did all these women know? Clea was not one to be discreet with her own or anyone's innermost secrets.

What a fool I've been. Jane bit her lip, praying the wave of tears would hold until she closed the door on all of them. Undoubtedly Alex suspected how she felt about him, and had used Clea to disabuse her once and for all time. How could he feel anything more than pity for her, too gauche, too inexperienced to know what a bore she must be with her impossible ambitions? What was she doing trafficking with all these people? She barely understood what they chattered about. What she knew about society she learned from Patrick and Madge, and it was to her an unrelieved picture of jaded people with too much money and too much time to indulge every kind of perverted pleasure.

Was all this sudden candor on Clea's part Alex's way of making the final payment on his obligation to Patrick? Madge was right. She had no business with anyone as debauched as Clea Wesley.

"I think, Lady Clea, I am much too tired to work today," she said.

Lady Clea agreed. "I am well satisfied. Do come and see your handiwork unveiled next week," she said, a mischievous look in her feral eyes.

"Now, my ladies, please retire to my house for tea. But first, you must do as I do."

Jane watched horrified, as Clea opened her reticule, taking out a handful of flimsies and placing them on the table, while the others followed suit. Still shaken by

Clea's admission of her affair with Alex, Jane didn't know what to make of this latest extraordinary scene: society women searching frantically for money and borrowing from each other.

"Please, I can wait," Jane said, on the point of bursting into tears. Was this a further attempt on Clea's part to embarrass and put her in her place?

Clea returned from shepherding her friends out of the studio.

"I shocked you about my affair with Alex, didn't I?"

"Of course not."

"Are we going to be brave?"

Clea forced Jane to face her.

"You are in love with Alex Barrington, aren't you?"

"Forgive me, Lady Clea, but my feelings are my own, and need not concern you. Obviously you know my situation, and your patronage has been enormously helpful, but I'll be damned before I become your friend or your confidante."

"How much do you love Alex?"

Jane stared and couldn't speak. It was a mistake. She had ruined any chance to lie. She loved Alex with all her heart, even as she hated him for making her vulnerable to feelings she had never known, confusing her devotion to her ambitions with the cravings of her body.

"I don't need an answer," Clea crowed.

Jane saw the triumph in Clea's eyes. She had to get away and moved toward the door.

Clea followed quickly and took Jane's arm, attempting to detain her. Her eyes glistened with mischief.

"How would you like to share a bed with Alex and me?"

Chapter Twenty-nine

James Manley waved a heavy vellum letter across the breakfast table.

"Alex Barrington made history in Scotland the day after he arrived. He caught a seventy-four-pound salmon. Would have given my right leg to be there, wouldn't I just?" he hooted.

Jane cringed. The last thing she wanted to hear was word that the Earl of Trent was alive, much less a hero. Her head was thick with lack of sleep, her eyes gritty. Damn Clea Wesley. Damn her soul. Jane wanted to go directly to the studio, but breakfast had become a ritual, and Jane never disappointed Manley if she could help it. Thankfully, Madge never rose before nine and breakfasted off a tray like all her London friends.

"The largest I ever heard of at Mr. Grove's in Bond Street was eighty-three pounds."

Manley looked over to see if Jane was listening.

She nodded, keeping her eyes averted. It wouldn't do for her canny host to see the ravages of the dilemma she was fighting: Tell Clea to go to the devil, and lose her friends and future commissions, or try to make peace and become nothing less than a spectacular *whore*. A lovely fate all around.

"Alex found him in a deep and rocky bed in a narrow ravine at the foot of Ben Cruachan. I know the place. It runs rapid and turbulent. Still, Alex caught the fellow on the second thrust, running out eighty yards of line with such speed that Alex was dragged over a mile of rocks and stones without stopping and a mile back. Took Alex all day, until he fell asleep and finally reeled the salmon in the next morning. Homeric it was!"

"Fish story," Jane remarked, absently imagining a picture of Alex exhausted on the bank to add to all the other sketches she secreted away in the studio and her bedroom. "Why didn't he just give up? Running down a stream for miles. Insanity."

"Alex is a fabulous angler. He wouldn't give up so easily."

"Blarney. Male stubbornness."

Manley laughed, lowered his eyeglasses, and peered across the table.

"Stubborn, is it? And what do you call your working eighteen hours at your easel, northern light or dark of night? Isn't that a titanic struggle? And now catering to someone like Clea Wesley? And what about a husband?" he asked cautiously.

Jane squirmed under his piercing glance.

"We'll see." *Never*, is what she almost said, but that would not do. It would only lead to more discussion she didn't want now, of all times.

"Whatever troubles you, Jane, it isn't ambition alone. I know that. When you care to tell me, I will listen."

With that he rose and left the dining room, his feet dragging on the Turkish carpet.

Jane pushed her plate aside, wondering how much he suspected. Were her secret longings for Alex not very secret after all? Madge talked of James's prowess with women as a young man. Jane was beginning to believe it never left him.

Jane reached for the post beside her plate, and walked to the garden. Another letter from Patrick with a brave face on matters at Dairty Hall. Another circular from Ackermann's, where she bought her supplies, but no letter from Alex Barrington. What did she expect?

Chapter Thirty

Jane stood in the middle of Clea Wesley's morning room in the most fashionable street in London, frozen with rage. She had been hanging about for half an hour, and the wait seemed interminable.

The fragile hold Jane had on her nerves was fast running out. But much as she wanted to, Jane dared not leave. It had been hard enough to summon the courage to make the journey.

Jane had long since finished her survey of the delightful room and its surprises. Unlike Clea's flash and dash, the simple, tasteful, blue-and-white wallpaper, matching window hangings, and country chairs were warm and in the best taste. At any other time Jane would have given anything to spend an hour over a cup of tea and explore the few small paintings arranged on the walls. They were exceptional, and hung with a knowing hand. Jane, had much experience studying Madge's collection of British art and criticism, the only library open to her when she was a child and the only education she had had in the history of art.

Jane walked to the window seeking another distraction from her impatience. How in the world did a simple Irish woman like herself ever get embroiled in such a lurid state of affairs.

To still her roiling mind she went back to studying the two rare Reynolds and Lawrence landscapes and a small Constable she and Madge had seen on sale only two weeks before. Obviously Clea had purchased them. Soon a door clicked open behind her. She turned, expecting to see Clea.

"Her ladyship has been delayed and will join you shortly," the butler announced and left. It was the second time he had made the same promise to her.

Jane sat down on a chair and laced her shaking fingers in her lap. Was she never going to see the end of her torment? It had been a week since Clea had turned her life on end. Every morning she woke tangled in her bed linen from salacious images she couldn't escape.

"Jane, my dear, so nice you have forgiven me," Clea called out, preceded by a mist of scent and clinging primrose silk. "Come and see how prettily I have had your nice study of me framed."

Jane was struck by the power and malevolence Clea exuded. "I think, Lady Clea, it would serve no purpose. I have managed to survive your attempt to shock me. However I cannot be of any further service to you, and I see no reason why you should feel a need to further my career."

"You are a fool. You need money, and I can help. I have already. Without me you will end like all the other hacks who come begging for my influence."

"Hack?"

Clea waved her off as if the question were not a death sentence.

"Your work has a certain flair and some skill, but you will never be first-rate. The trouble with you is that you have higher aspirations than talent, a common malady. I come across it every day. With me, you will have cachet. 'Clea's new protégée.' But when I drop you, and you can be sure I will, everyone else will follow me. Don't play the stupid virgin with me. The true artists I know are not in the least adverse to adventurous bedroom frolics," Clea said, laughing at Jane.

"Think of a threesome in Alex's bed or an alternative I've decided might suit me more. Enter into a marriage of convenience with Alex. He has no desire to produce an heir himself. And if you keep out of his bed, I will move heaven and earth to make you famous and rich in your own right."

Jane stared, unbelieving, at Clea and this latest outrage.

"I know naked ambition when I see it," Clea went on. "And I know London's foibles and how to play on them. I intend to keep Alex, whatever comes. You interest him for some strange reason, but I will move heaven and earth to keep him. With Alex and me, you can have all you ever want."

Jane smoothed her gloves, took a deep breath. Naive, stupid, or otherwise, she knew her own mind.

"You may know art, my dear Lady Clea, but you don't know me. The Earl of Trent may be sympathetic to me, but only as a favor to my brother. He has no designs on me, and I have none on him. Hardly. I detest the man!"

Chapter Thirty-one

The remnants of a heavy meal lay on the huge, blackened oak table, with Alex and his friends slumped in throne-like chairs in various stages of drunkenness.

"Fire." Burner reeled to his feet and proposed still another toast to Alex's salmon.

"Dear God, not again," Alex pleaded.

Cheers went up in support of his protest, but didn't stop their host.

At any other time, Alex, who prided himself on his skill as a fisherman, would have enjoyed basking in the admiration of his friends, all sportsmen of the first rank. His feat—and it was a feat, he supposed—would probably become part of local lore, but that mattered little to him at the moment. And for that he could blame a black-haired, smudged-faced, stubborn lass, who had succeeded in turning his life upside-down and sideways.

He had been miserable from the first moment he had left London and arrived in a Scottish downpour that seldom abated. He was restless and broody.

"You've made me and my loch famous, and I'll soon be overrun by poachers," Fire said, with a great sigh.

Alex took the toast and sank back in now-familiar gloom. He didn't want to see another salmon, or hear another damned fish story for as long as he lived. Sick of the interminable cold and wet, tired of the endless wasted hours, he had had enough of himself. London held all he wanted in the person of Jane Daitry, talking in her fevered way about her painting. Where were his eyes when he had first spied her in Ireland? Couldn't he see the wonderful woman behind the poverty and despair? No, he was too busy planning to ruin his colonel's life and his own career in the bargain.

A lot of good pining for what he couldn't have did him. By now John Lear was back in London planning a wedding to the woman that should have been his. Alex sat bold upright. He had admitted it. Love! Marriage! Magically, it wasn't the bugaboo he had dreaded for so long. What a turnabout! The alternative, the possibility of becoming another James Manley, if he didn't watch out, suddenly appalled him.

Out of the din, he heard his name called.

"Drink up," Fire bellowed down the long expanse of table, his eyes swimming in the good Scottish whiskey he consumed like water. "Alex, when did you get to be such a serious fellow? You're a bloody pall on my party."

"Serious, am I?" Alex called out as he shook off his malaise. He leapt out of his chair, pulled a crossed broadsword from the wall, and mounted the table. "I've chosen my weapon, Fire. What account will you give of yourself?"

Roaring his acceptance, Burner took up the challenge. He rose and pulled off the remaining broadsword. The two met well matched and parried along the length of the table, spraying dishes, glasses, and cutlery in their wake. Down the hall went the drunken combatants, up the broad stairs, with the others cheering them on, in and out of bedrooms, galleries, and long, gloomy corridors, striking sparks, almost dismembering each other, giving pleasure and concern along the way. The mock sword fight went on all over the massive castle, until they returned to the dining hall and collapsed, drunken and spent, their feet in the dying fire and whiskey bottles emptying down their parched throats.

"You win, Alex," Burner conceded. "You're not boring. You're a goddamned madman."

Alex arrived last for breakfast the next morning, and immediately sickened at the sight of the vast varieties and amount of uneaten food arrayed on the sideboards. His conscience rose up like bile. He feasted while his Legion starved. He asked for beer, cheese, and digestive biscuits.

"I say, a bit invalidish, are we?" Burner called out cheerfully, waving a slab of ham speared at the end of his fork. "Heartburn or missing Clea?"

The rest took up the refrain, and Alex waited for the jeering to subside.

"Where is the post?" he asked. "Roads can't be flooded out this long." He was glad to see others had the same complaint.

"Norris, where's the damn mail," Burner called to his butler. "You said a lad had been sent."

"Letters and newspapers are being ironed," a footman offered and left the dining room on the run.

A few minutes later a small boy carrying a wicker basket arrived, and was nearly mobbed.

Alex recognized Lear's handwriting, and his heart stopped. He put his letter on the bottom of the pile. What he imagined in the letter—happy wedding plans—was bad enough; confirmation was worse. Instead he took up a letter marked with James Manley's seal.

"Dear Barrington:
Lear will have told you what happened. I am most concerned about Jane. She paints furiously to satisfy all the patronesses Lady Clea Wesley has introduced to her.

"As you may imagine, my sister is in shock.

"I fear painting fashionable ladies to make money is ruining her talent.

"With John Lear's defection, you must help me arrange another marriage for Jane."

Alex tore into the letter from Lear.

"Dear Alex:

"I hope you will understand that I never wanted this to happen. Lady Jane and I have mutually and amicably broken off our betrothal . . ."

Alex smiled and folded the letters carefully.

He called across the table. "Sorry, chaps, I have urgent business in London, and must leave at once."

Chapter Thirty-two

"Brilliant," James Manley said, glancing over six unfinished canvases. He had come to say good night to Jane.

"Insipid I call them, and so will anyone else if they're ever displayed."

"Certainly not," he said, stricken by the desperation he saw in Jane's dark-rimmed eyes.

"I have it on very good authority."

"Whose?"

Jane turned, prepared to tell him. Then she bit her lip and thought better of it. "It's not important. I will finish them all, collect my fees, and a noble experiment gone amiss will be mercifully over."

Manley's heart lifted. "I can't wait to see the last of Clea Wesley and that thundering herd of hers."

Jane went back to her palette, hiding her hands. They were shaking like the palsy, and had been since her late unpleasantness with Clea.

"You have made vast strides for someone so young and new to London," Manley said consolingly. "You've proven you can attract patrons. Now is the time to follow your heart. Go and settle with Claude Morgan."

Jane resumed working, fighting off an almost overwhelming need to confide all the shocks Clea had administered to her fragile confidence and simple Irish morals. In a few well-delivered barbs, the Lady Clea had reduced her to the same aspen leaf she used to see in her mirror in Ireland. This is what happened, she thought harshly, when someone dared to want more than her portion and displeased the gods.

An artist? What a laugh.

Hopelessly infatuated with Alexander Barrington? What a fool.

How could she—though she wanted so much to tell him all it made her teeth ache—admit to James Manley, of all people, how she almost, in the dark of night, sold herself to become Clea and Alex's bedmate, or anything else they wanted of her? Almost sold her artist's honor to a flock of aging, giddy women who wanted her to erase the wounds of riotous living in her portraits of them.

Of all the people she had met since coming to London, Uncle James was the only one who never seemed to waver in his affection and support of everything she wanted in life. She had never had anything but frigid silence and neglect from her father. What little warmth she had had from any man came from Patrick, but he was seldom about when she needed him.

"Jane, shall I go?" Manley asked.

She found him watching her from the depths of an armchair on the side of her easel, his eyes heavy with concern for her. She hated bringing so much disquiet into his and Madge's once-placid lives. They denied it was so, but she knew it to be true.

Jane put down the brush and kissed Manley on the cheek. Then arm in arm they walked back to the house.

"All this will be over soon," Jane said, turning him over to the butler. "I will be myself as soon as I finish with the last of my commissions."

Manley saluted her and went to his room, feeling old and useless. Where the hell was Alex? Surely he knew by now that Jane and Lear were not betrothed. Yet he had given no sign that it made the slightest difference and remained "among his salmon," as Jane called the remote castle in Scotland.

If he was wrong about Alex, was he wrong about Jane and her feelings for Alex? After she had refused Lear, Jane had become positively radiant, light of step, singing in the house and the studio. He felt confident enough to write to Scotland, hoping to elicit Alex's immediate return. However, he'd been wrong before, and it looked as if he was wrong again.

Chapter Thirty-three

Alex Barrington strode toward Hanover Square whistling tunelessly, like a lovesick barrow boy, swinging his silver-headed cane, his hat at a rakish tilt. He was trying to instill a jauntiness that escaped him completely the nearer he came to Jane's studio.

His hair was still wet from a hasty bath to wash away the grime of a horrendously long and frustrating trip from Scotland. His face still burned where Atkins had shaved him within an inch of his life while clucking over the mattress-thick hair Alex had grown in the highlands.

Time seemed to creep by, and Alex dawdled at home until it was safe to depart. It would not do to arrive too early and risk a chance meeting with Madge Brooks or her brother, on this of all nights.

He left his house, rehearsing all the ways he was going to ask Jane to marry him, but the closer he came, the less certain he was that he wanted to marry. Hard-held habits of a lifetime were difficult to change, even if a dark-eyed, dark-haired houri captivated him without a wile or art to her name. If she had refused good, reliable John Lear, what chance had he? Was he ready for marriage? Did he want a wonderful, if sometimes difficult, woman or any woman in his life? Was it fair to saddle poor Jane with someone as unsettled and mercurial as he?

Alex went to the garden door, then walked in circles until he thought he would go mad. He came to offer for Jane, and here he was dithering like a cowherd. In for a penny, in for a pound. With that thought he threw a few coins over the brick wall to attract the watchman's attention, and waited for him to unbolt the door. He tipped the man, and walked toward the studio, his hands clammy and his heart doing somersaults in his chest.

More candles than usual turned night into day. He opened the studio door and waited for Jane to see him. She was, as always, lost in a world of her own, everything about her concentrated, shoulders and lithe body leaning into the easel as if she would climb into the canvas and wring life out of it. He had never forgotten what Jane had said about hating a white canvas.

He saw her arch her back, massage her neck, and suddenly throw down the brush she'd been using, cursing with magnificent fluency in English and what he supposed was Gaelic. Tears rolled down her face. She wiped them away angrily with hands stained by paint, and pivoted, and he saw that her eyes were dull with fatigue and something else he'd never seen before. Despair?

She saw him standing just inside the door.

"You bastard."

Alex burst out laughing, easily evading a heavy trowel sailing toward his head. "What have I done now?"

"Everything. You sent Clea to feed my vanity and make me her court painter," she hissed at him. "And then you had her ask me to share a bed with the two of you."

He had no difficulty recognizing Clea's fine Italian hand brewing trouble.

"Even for Clea that's a monstrous suggestion," he said, the laughter dead in him. "If you believed me capable of seconding such a thing, then you have learned nothing about me, and that concerns me terribly."

She stalked toward him and they bent to retrieve the tool at the same moment, their heads almost colliding, so close their breaths intermingled. His hands reached out to help her to her feet. She lost her balance and seemed to lean into him. He pulled her into his arms and kissed her as she struggled within his grasp.

All indecision faded. He wanted more than the innocence and camaraderie of the long, rambling hours in the studio before he left for Scotland. He held her close. She fought him. He kissed her long and felt her fear.

"Trust me. I won't ever hurt you." He would be patient, fight for her, and watch over her, treading carefully until she could return his love. But first she had to fulfill her dreams. He would follow wherever they took her.

Once on her feet, Jane wrenched free of him. All the loneliness of his absence, all the newfound confidence in herself that Clea had destroyed disappeared with his touch. She wanted to fight him, but knew she would succumb, wanted to succumb to the fever that Alex brought to her. Inexplicably, he released her. She was confused, but hid it perfectly. She had a moment to come to her senses, and she wouldn't lose them again. She backed away.

Alex smiled and returned the trowel to her, keeping as far away as he could. It was going to be hell, but he would wait for her to come to him of her own will when she was ready to do so.

"Now tell me what other mischief has Clea made with you while I froze in Scotland?"

Jane went back to her easel, shaking in every limb but trying to appear untroubled. Love? Impossible. Not for her. She daubed at the canvas until she could speak without giving herself away.

"Clea thinks I am a hack and has withdrawn her support," she said bleakly. "And, of course, she is right."

"Surely you didn't believe her? She was trying to hurt you for refusing her plans for you," he said savagely. "Thank heaven you didn't stop painting."

"There is a lot to be said for needing money. Much as I wanted to throw everything away, I must complete these and be paid the money I earned."

Alex hated to be the one to burst that pretty bubble.

"You'll never be paid. Clea will see to that. Forget it. You want to be a miniaturist? Be the best you can. Lose yourself in what you really want, and put all this behind you."

A sudden, terrible chill forced Jane to wrap her arms around her shoulders. Could she believe in herself again? Did she have the talent for anything?

Alex took an old shawl from a heap of clothes Jane kept nearby and tried to put it around her shoulders. Jane backed away clumsily.

"Thank you, but I do not require your help," she said, snatching the shawl. How could she bear a repetition of what went on before, still feeling raw and naked.

"Forget Clea. Put yourself to the test with Morgan. I did you a terrible turn allowing Clea to get within a mile of you. I should have known better." He would ring Clea's neck the next time he saw her.

"And now, my lord, I thank you for your concern, but I must get back to work."

She turned her back on him.

Helpless, Alex started to leave when a last thought occurred to him. Was part of her despair not only the result of Clea, but her broken betrothal as well?

"I neglected to say how sorry I am to hear that you and John Lear are no longer betrothed."

Jane turned around and faced him.

"You need not trouble yourself about that, my lord," she said airily. "Your attempts to buy me a husband failed. John Lear now knows how fortunate he is. I have no interest in matrimony, and never did. I don't need anyone."

"I am sorry to hear that," Alex said, trying to hide the real distress he felt. What a fool he was to suspect he could ever make a difference to this woman. "I used to think I didn't need anyone, and I can tell you I found I was wrong. You must learn that for yourself."

"With respect, my lord, I lived all my life fending for myself. It was a wondrous lesson."

She walked to the door and held it open for him.

"I won't leave until you explain." He felt he had stumbled on to something that might tell him why this strange woman wanted nothing from anyone.

"You know more than enough about me, more than I like, but I will tell you this," Jane said in a cold, emphatic voice. "You and everyone think I am wrong to desire to be a great miniaturist. They mean more to me than little pictures that can be easily transported. They can be a lifeline."

Alex left, feeling depleted. He had accomplished nothing.

Chapter Thirty-four

Jane stood before the tiny, white-timbered house with the black shutters, afraid to sound the bell.

"God hates a coward, Lizzie," she said at last. Pulling her maid along, Jane pushed open the gate hanging off the hinges, and marched up the small, overgrown front garden. With a bit of paint and weeding, the little house just off South Audley Street could be more inviting than the large Georgian mansions dwarfing it.

She looked for a door pull and found none. She nudged the door with her foot, and it opened with much creaking. The smell was overwhelming, and she and Lizzie coughed in unison.

"Come in, if you're coming, or stay the hell out," a rough voice called out.

Jane and Lizzie exchanged wary glances and entered.

If the outside of the house was uninviting, the inside was appalling.

"Who are you, and what do you want?"

"I am Lady Jane Daitry, and this is my maid, Elizabeth. I wrote to you for an appointment."

"You didn't say you were a peeress, just you were a serious painter," Claude Morgan said, looking Jane and Lizzie over with undisguised disinterest. "I don't take la de da ladies who want to make pretty miniatures. Stick to painting dishes with all the other women who play at art. I'll be hanged if I'll waste my genius."

"I need to make a living, sir. I don't play at painting.

Tell me how much I need to pay for lessons, and let us begin."

Reeking of raw whiskey bought with money better spent on soap and water for himself and his house, Morgan held out two crooked hands bound in dirty gloves, his yellowed brown eyes staring at Jane's reticule.

"What have you there?"

"Twenty pounds." Jane held her breath. Despite her extreme parsimony, she had little left of Patrick's money. Alex had been right, of course. Clea's friends had refused her sketches, and she was left worse off than before. Teachers as good as Morgan, despite his unprepossessing appearance, were expensive Besides, she hadn't time to scurry about London looking for anyone else. She had to make the most of the month left before Madge returned to Ireland. She couldn't afford a place of her own, and she couldn't continue to accept Uncle James's hospitality, no matter how much he insisted.

"Two pounds for looking at that portfolio your maid's carrying," Morgan cackled, and rolled his chair toward the back.

They followed, and Jane's spirits lifted. The airy room was a studio of sorts, tidier and far more inviting than the rest of the place.

He took a second pound from the flimsies Jane had given him.

"You. What's your name? Go to the tavern on the corner, pay what I owe on the slate, and bring back all the gin the landlord will give you."

Lizzie left as soon as Jane assured her she would be fine, impatient for Morgan to see her work and agree to take her on. Jane couldn't remember when she had felt more frightened and hopeful. The dream of her life might actually be realized in the next few minutes. She walked, weak-legged, to a window and waited for the old artist to finish looking at her work.

"Have you ever had a painting lesson, for God's sake?" Morgan sneered, holding one picture after the other to the light and sailing them across the room at Jane's feet.

"A few itinerant painters came through Craig Bay and gave me lessons, sir."

"You're no Angelica Kauffmann, but you have some small originality. I never had a lesson in my life. Now take off your coat and hat and make me something to eat. The slut who does for me is angry with me and won't be coming for a few days. There's something in the larder. You and your maid can feast off a cart up the street."

"Then you will take me on?"

"I'll give you three weeks to convince me you know which end of a brush is which," he said grinning, showing a row of rotten teeth.

Jane's stomach turned. Everything about the man and his house made her want to flee. He might be dirty and fierce, but Clea said he was one of the best teachers in London, and cheap. She must remember that. She needed Morgan more than he appeared to want to teach her.

Lizzie appeared with an apronful of bottles. Jane knew Morgan wasn't smiling at her, but at the spirits her maid carried into the room.

"Be here at seven to make my breakfast, and we'll start at eight. I'll work your hands raw. I curse like a bandit. If you become missish, I'll throw you out, and that's the last you'll see of me or your money. Agreed? If your maid must be with you, she'll act as my char-woman and your model, though she has a face only a mother could love."

Lizzie bristled and appealed silently to Jane.

"Mr. Morgan, you can say what you will about me, but you'll be civil to my maid. Is that understood?"

He cackled, upended one of the bottles that Lizzie brought, and dismissed them out of hand.

In the brilliant sunshine, Jane laughed aloud as she pulled Lizzie along with her.

"I'm to be a professional miniaturist, and then back to Ireland. Lizzie, be happy for me," Jane cried. "Please."

Chapter Thirty-five

Alex arrived at Manley House and was shown into the drawing room, where Madge Brooks presided over a majestic tea service. He accepted a delicate Wedgewood cup and sat on a sofa facing her.

"You said in your note you had some questions you hoped I would answer," Madge said, her voice cold.

"You've known the Daitry family for years, and perhaps you can tell me things that puzzle me," Alex started, giving her a smile he had reason to believe was pleasing to his mother's contemporaries.

It worked again. At once Madge seemed less hostile, indeed almost smiled back at him.

"Jane's mother and I were best friends."

"Then you can help me!"

Madge Brooks examined her beringed fingers.

"I don't know how much Jane and Patrick would approve my telling you. They are the proudest pair of purse-poor aristocrats in a country that grows that sort."

"As I well know. To show you I am sincere in my inquiries, I will tell you a secret. Two weeks ago my man of business purchased all the mortgages on the Daitry estate. He will quite suddenly find it in his heart to advance Patrick enough money to begin extensive repairs."

Madge Brooks put down her teacup and studied the pattern on her cup.

"Why are you doing this?"

"Patrick was one of the young officers under my command, and I heard recently, not from Jane you can be sure, that he is hopelessly bankrupt. I may still not meet with your approval, Mrs. Brooks, but I always take care of my own." It wouldn't do to tell a stiff-necked tartar—the self-appointed guardian of Jane's virtue and future—the truth. She'd have apoplexy if she knew how much he loved Jane and would fight the devil himself to have her.

"I think you are entitled to answers to any questions you want to put to me," Madge said, taking out her handkerchief. "Thomas Daitry was the most selfish, indulgent wastrel I ever met. To my certain knowledge, the only clothes and toys Patrick and Jane ever had came from me. And even then, I was only allowed to give them presents at birthdays. I envied them their Patrick and Jane. I was, unfortunately, barren."

Alex moved over to sit beside her, and took her hand in his.

"The Daitry children were brought up without supervision or concern. The servants were lazy, but loyal, and saw to the minimum comfort of the children. They were wild and charming, and my husband and I adored them."

Madge poured more tea in their cups and smiled warmly at Alex.

"Thomas fought with everyone, didn't know a thing about horses, but fancied himself the best horse and hound man in Ireland. To be stupid is one thing. To be arrogant as well is disaster. Then he started to drink the day around, and managed to make an enemy of every decent man in Craig Bay and fifty miles away." Madge recounted her story in a hard, angry voice. "None of the best families would have anything to do with them. He alienated everyone. Yet Sheila loved him to distraction, and took to her bed as soon as all the money was gone. Except for my husband and myself, the children were isolated from polite society for most of their young lives."

"Is that when Jane began painting?"

"I remember seeing Jane in their dreary drawing room copying the family miniatures for hours on end. She showed me houses and clothes she'd made and wove stories about them. Very inventive she was, even then. She always studied my collection the way most children read storybooks. She made excellent copies of all of them. Once I found mine arrayed in their drawing room with a set of clothes made from rags. That must have been after Thomas had sold all of theirs. The Daitry collection was a much larger and more valuable collection than mine, now that I think on it," Madge said sadly.

"I don't recollect seeing them when I visited." Alex remembered the house as devoid of any pictures, not even anything by Jane. "Where did the money come from to send Patrick to Eton and buy him a commission in the Guards?"

"My husband. He had to knock Thomas down to do it. But they never let us do as much for Jane. Sheila was completely dependent on her after Thomas died. She was, I regret to say, a selfish woman."

Alex took Madge's hand again and placed a light kiss on it.

"Thank you for being so helpful."

He stood up, about to say good-bye, when James Manley came into the room. He was wreathed in smiles, and Alex noted his clothes were unusually tidy and fashionable. He also seemed to have discarded one of his two walking sticks.

"I heard you were here, and you are the very man I wanted to see." Manley took a seat next to him. "Madge, be a dear. Would you ask Barrett to have some fresh tea and scones sent up to us. I wish to have a long 'coze,' as you women like to say, with Barrington."

His sister took the hint, smiled, and just before she quit the room added, "I think, Alexander, you and I cleared away years of misunderstanding, and I am well pleased to tell you so." She smiled warmly and left them.

"I say, what did you do to old Madge? She was positively glowing."

"I think I have proved I have the Daitrys' well-being at heart."

"I never doubted it, dear boy," Manley said heartily, and lit a cigar. "I have some news for you. Jane's birthday is soon, and I have decided to give a slap-up party for her. This place has been a tomb for thirty years, but I am throwing an army into freshening the whole house."

Alex listened politely, unsure why any of this should concern him.

"Madge is going to ask Sally Jersey to help collect six of the most eligible men in London and an equal number of young ladies," he said smugly. "A bit of our own Marriage Mart, you might say."

Alex wasn't sure he liked the sound of the party. But if Jane wasn't interested in him, he had no right to interfere in any plan her friends made to marry her well.

"And lest you think men won't be climbing all over themselves to propose to a penniless Irish gel, I will let it be known that I have made Jane independently wealthy."

"My God, you're in love with Jane yourself."

"Not quite." The old man sighed. "You see, she has given me a new interest in life. No daughter or granddaughter could have been kinder or more loving. None would have asked less of me."

"And if none of the men come up to scratch?"

"I'll offer her marriage, in name only, of course! She will have my name and my money. She'll never want for anything. As far as the world is concerned, Jane will not be a spinster."

"You will marry her?" Alex asked in a strangled voice.

"Yes. But only a marriage of convenience."

Shocked, Alex put down his teacup and rose to leave.

Behind him James Manley smiled to himself. If nothing else, he'd given Alex Barrington something to think about.

Chapter Thirty-six

Jane's head rested on Claude Morgan's scarred, slant-topped miniaturist's desk, more miserable than she had ever been in her life.

These last few weeks had been hellish. She hadn't drawn the first line to please the old man, and was afraid her money and her strength would run out before she did. She slept less than ever, and when she did, she suffered nightmares of failure after failure, with Morgan's face a gargoyle continuously jeering at her.

"What have you done since I left you?" Morgan roared at her, wheeling back into the room in a haze of stale gin, a new bottle clutched between his twisted fingers.

"You haven't learned a blessed thing," he roared, throwing a just-completed study of Lizzie across the cluttered room.

"I'm wasting my time! I taught Robertson all he knows. I was the first to do away with the benighted pink cheeks and lips and the blue beards so loved by the old guard," he stormed at her. "I made my work true to life, introduced warmth and harmony. I brought delicacy of color to the old, raddled ladies and dyspeptic generals and m'lords, and I end up teaching a dunderhead like you."

She heard his boasting in her sleep, and barely listened as he continued the same litany.

"What the *ton* foams at the mouth over in Andrew

Robertson and his brothers in America, I did without credit years ago," he bellowed in a voice coarsened by drink. "I was always particular with my drawing, faithful to correct form, a true likeness, expression, sentiment, and made character the heart of the picture. I introduced bolder colors, gave my sitters more humanity."

"I quite agree, sir, but what am I doing wrong? I have reproduced your very own copies of Sir Henry Raeburn, but you won't even look at them," Jane wailed, and disliked the sound of it. "I can never have your gifts, but why can't I please you?"

"Please me? The man whose watercolors were so original, so perfect, it was thought by some to be oils? You dare compare yourself to me and want to please me?"

Crazed with drink, Morgan twisted her words, spat at her, called her every idiot under the sun. Often he confused her with pupils of earlier years, and slashed the few efforts she'd been able to finish on ivory or vellum with a crop he carried across his lap. She endured every indignity, every oath, mindful she had no money to go to anyone else. Time was running out. Madge would soon be returning to Ireland. With John Lear back in Yorkshire wooing his Margaret, no one else had appeared on the scene to sweep her off her feet and offer her a way out of this unremitting hell. It was a measure of the depths she had descended to that even marriage seemed an attractive release from the hell she was in.

Yet for all his twisted ego and miserable temperament, Claude Morgan was beyond doubt the towering, unsung genius and original he claimed to be. She'd found this to be true a few days earlier, when she had come upon an open closet and had found a dozen dusty, unframed miniatures of the same woman, so luminous, so alive and pure she wanted to weep. It made her face herself as never before. She could never touch Morgan's talent, no matter how long she worked with him or anyone else. She was a fool, and no amount of dreaming, praying, and sacrifice would change the facts.

Morgan found her so rapt in her admiration that she forgot the time. He raised the crop over his head, but Jane stayed her ground, one of the few times she did not quake before his ire.

"Why do you hide them? They are your immortality. At least exhibit them," she implored him. "Remind people you are still alive. Or sell them, and live a life of ease with the proceeds."

"Mind your own business."

"Who is the woman? She is magnificent."

"She was my wife. They are all I have of her. Go away. You bore me. You have no magic in your hands."

Jane left to find her cape.

"Get back to work," he said, blocking her way.

She did, but continued to feel on the edge of dread and flight. Worn and dismayed, day and night were the same: tongue lashings from Morgan, doubts of her ability chilling and stiffening her fingers, riven by alternating pictures of exquisite moments in Alex's arms and Morgan harassing her; moments of excruciating panic and fear over and over again.

Today she was remembering all this, when Morgan, drunker than usual, threw an empty bottle against the fireplace, and arching shards grazed her foot beneath the table.

"No matter how much your high and mighty fancy man pays me, you are never going to be any good. You are capable. Stick with your portraits. You can get away with murder there."

Jane flew out of the chair, knocking the desk off the table.

"What did you say?"

Morgan leered at her, and held out a rumpled calling card from his waistcoat. The Earl of Trent. You aim high, Lady Irish."

Jane pushed his hand aside.

"You're hopeless. You are ham-handed. You needed lessons from a master years ago. You've formed bad habits. You are nothing."

Morgan rolled his chair across the room, where he kept his rogue's gallery of miniatures by what he called "third-raters." They were names Jane recognized and thought of as artists of some standing.

"Mediocrity is a curse. The world is contaminated with bad art, and worse, bad artists," he said, his words slurred, his head beginning to sink to his chest. "You're not a bad portrait painter. You have the merit of originality—better than some I could name. Stay with what you do best. You are a third-rate miniaturist. Go away."

Jane struggled to her feet and gathered her things with her last ounce of strength.

"Be content. Get married. Have babies. But stop fooling yourself," he boomed as she struggled to the door. "You don't have a God-given gift. It is bestowed on only a few."

Jane called out for Lizzie to come to her.

"Bloody Martin Shee is right. Many of my fellow miniaturists are lazy, safe blockheads with little ambition or higher aspirations, painting away for quick pounds and pence, while geniuses like me molder. The Quality suck our blood and blacken our names, because we dare to ask to be paid. I spent twenty-two hours doing one bitch, prostituting myself, giving her character and dignity she did not have. It was the last commission I ever received."

Jane paused at the door, watching tears splatter down Morgan's chest and over the bottles he cradled in his withered arms. Jane wanted to weep and scream for him. She did neither. For herself, the house of ambition, the aspirations of greatness that had sustained her for so long were rubble at her feet.

Chapter Thirty-seven

Alex sat at the card table at Crockford's, stacks of vowels and chips piled half as high as the etched brandy glass beside them.

His luck over the past few weeks had proved phenomenal, the talk of the clubs, and men flocked to the tables hoping to see for themselves if Alex's luck was real and catching.

For Alex, it had become the only way to mark time. Jane refused to see him, Lear was in Yorkshire planning a winter wedding, and the Legion's business was doing splendidly. For the first time in his life, the Earl of Trent was bored to the teeth.

Counting the days until Jane felt secure as a miniaturist and left Claude Morgan, and judging the propitious moment to make her an offer were wreaking havoc with his sleep. He wanted Jane as he had never wanted any woman, wavering between supreme joy and deep misery. At the moment he felt magnanimous about the mounds of money before him and ordered champagne for everyone.

When he bent over to rake in another small fortune, Atkins appeared at his elbow and whispered in his ear. Alex sprung up, knocking his chair to the ground.

"I must go. Cash me in," he called over his shoulder.

A horse awaited him at the door of the club, and he swung into the saddle. He arrived at James Manley's house within minutes.

The garden door swung open at his approach, and he raced to the studio. Manley was wringing his hands.

"Alex, do something, please."

Alex opened the door and was rocked on his heels.

Wielding a knife, crying hysterically, Jane was cutting and slashing her way through her work of the last months.

"Stop. It's a massacre," he said, grappling with her. She was stronger than he anticipated. He had to grasp her hand and press hard, until she cried out and the ugly-looking knife fell to the ground.

"Why are you destroying everything you've slaved over?"

"I'm creating a graveyard."

"What!"

"A bad artist died today."

"Very dramatic, I'm sure."

"You bought Claude Morgan for me, only to tell me what I have known all along. I'm a failure."

"There are other teachers."

"I don't want other teachers. I'm finished." She pulled away and swayed. He caught her up in his arms and gentled her like a child. Soon the restraint of months dissolved, and he rocked back and forth, whispering in her hair all he had wanted to tell her, afraid he would never find the words or the opportunity again.

Jane wept and whimpered, until there were no tears left, and, with little strength remaining, fought her way out of his grasp.

"Go away. Leave me alone."

Alex fell back on his heels.

"You've done enough. First Clea, and then Morgan. How much can I take?"

He reached out and seized her hands, pulled her against his chest, all gentleness gone. He kissed her lips, forcing her mouth to open. His tongue held to hers. Jane moaned, and fell against him. They clung together, breathless and unmoving. He ran his hands through her hair, caressing her neck until her pulse raced under his fingertips, matching his own. He moved his leg between hers, with ever-increasing insinuation, moving back and forth, until Jane caught his rhythm, and they soared above the sky, appeasing appetites, crying for release. She was awakening to sensations she never dreamed of, her body melting into his, the world mercifully removed.

"Vixen," he breathed into her ear. "Marry me. Now."

Jane went slack against him.

"This is mad. Go away. Please go away," she demanded, all the disappointments of weeks crowding in on her. "I can't. I won't marry you."

He let her go, his heart racing, looking at her as if he'd never seen her before. He was trying to read and understand how a woman could fill his arms, return him heartbeat for heartbeat, her ardor equal to his, and a moment later push him away as if he had imagined it all.

Jane tried to turn away. "I don't want love. I don't want to be married to you, or anyone. Love maims. It killed my mother. Poor Verna yearns for Patrick's smile. And foolish Clea would grovel before the world to keep you by her. No thank you. I don't want love in my life."

"Jane, listen to me."

"No. I have nothing to give you, or anyone. I'm finished. A piece of me died today. I have nothing to give anyone."

Alex moved with panther grace around the studio, picking up the paintings that had been spared in the massacre. When he could trust his voice, he handed them to her.

"Here, finish the job. I love you. I've never said that to any woman, and I won't say it again, until you tell me you want to hear it," Alex said quietly. "I can give you a king's ransom in jewels, furs, and palaces, but I can never give you back the death of a lifetime of dreaming. No one can. But I would try."

"Leave me alone."

Alex looked around the studio, remembering all the hours he had spent learning about Jane, knowing he had lost.

Chapter Thirty-eight

Jane allowed Madge and Lizzie to dress her for her birthday party with the same cool detachment she did everything these last few weeks.

"Tell me you aren't thrilled with the way you look," Madge asked, forcing Jane to look at herself in a huge three-sided mirror. "You have become one of the most interesting women in London, my darling girl. Everyone says so."

At last Jane smiled and drew Madge into her arms. She had accomplished what she had set out to do, to please James and Madge in everything they asked of her. She had learned to listen without hearing and smile without mirth. They pushed and pulled in every direction. She made no objection to being fitted for a numbing and endless parade of gowns, being talked and lectured at, meeting hosts of people. She even met the holy of holies, Lady Sally Jersey, who gave Jane her blessings. All this without revealing how little she felt or cared.

Jane met every eligible man in London who came out of the woodwork when Madge Brooks let it drop among her bosom bows that James planned to settle a fortune on Jane. No man made an impression on her. None could touch the cold, formless calm that had at last come to fill the place where her hopeless ambitions had once lived. The studio was empty, a shell, very much like Jane herself.

Yet to her surprise, she was neither happy nor unhappy. She had survived. She dried her tears, stopped ranting against the Fates, and ceased grieving for the simple Jane Daitry who had come to London with hope that all too soon burned her fingers.

But more painful than anything was hardening her heart and body against the memory of Alex, the feel of his arms around her, the hellfire warmth he had created within her that night in the studio and that still charred her body day and night as she remembered what he could do to her.

The one surety she had that her memories of Alex would fade centered on the day after tomorrow, when she and Madge would return to Ireland. The circle would close, and she would be back at Daitry House and the anonymity she craved.

"Are you ready, my dear?"

Jane looked up and smiled. Aunt Madge and Uncle James stood at the door waiting to take her to the first birthday party she ever had in her life.

"Thank you, I'll find my way," Alex called over his shoulder to a footman who tried to block his way up the long, graceful stairway. He stood alone at the door of Manley's ballroom a few minutes before midnight.

Newly painted, breezes riffling through stiff, new curtains covering the floor-to-ceiling windows, the small ballroom blazed with candles. The scent of the most expensive flowers in London mingled with the tinkling of delicate glasses and laughter and strolling violins.

Alex stood in the doorway, unsure why he'd come when he had promised himself he wouldn't. Did he think showing up would magically change Jane's mind? His gifts and flowers were returned. The few times he came to call, he was turned away by the butler in the most regretful manner.

Still, Manley sent him an invitation and begged him to come.

His eyes swept the room and the dozen dazzling young men and women spread out before him, all dressed as Manley had commanded, in black-and-white evening costumes to match the new decor of the elegant ballroom.

"I did a rather good job of it, wouldn't you say?" James Manley said, clapping Alex on the back.

"It's only the most talked-about party of the day, and Jane the most talked-about heiress of the season," Alex conceded, knowing he would make the old man happy talking of Manley's great success. "How did you get her to take the money? Word of it has spread like wildflowers."

"It's a loan," Manley replied, laughing. "She plans to use some of it on Daitry House. Apparently you swore Patrick to secrecy. She doesn't know what you have done."

Alex nodded and peered into the crowd.

"I thought it was supposed to be her dowry?"

"You know Jane. She's the last one to hang out for a husband. I've done all I can. Ten marriage proposals in three weeks," Manley said proudly. "Where was yours?"

"She refused mine," Alex said, turning slowly to face Manley to see if he knew about the night in the studio. "She told me she wouldn't accept any offer, mine especially."

"Do something you fool," Manley muttered.

Alex turned and pumped Manley's hand.

This time when his gaze swept the guests in front of him, he looked for and found the most interesting woman in the room. Dressed in the simplest white Grecian gown, draped by a skilled hand over her slim hips and clinging suggestively to long, lean legs, Jane stood hauntingly alone, while all the men around her fought for her attention. Nearby, Sally Jersey talked to

Madge. Jane had arrived in London society. No doubt of it.

Alex's mouth was dry, and he walked stiffly with jangling nerves toward her. He hadn't felt so young and uncertain since his days as a junior officer at his first military ball.

Jane watched his progress and lost all interest in the conversation surrounding her. To her, Alex walked like a conqueror, tall, sure, as if the world belonged to him. It did. She missed him. Oh God, how she missed him.

"Lady Jane, will you dance with me on your birthday?"

"My card is full, my lord, but these gentlemen will allow one waltz for an old family friend." Jane smiled at her admirers and walked ahead of Alex. She raised her arms, her face a mask of supreme indifference.

Expecting a rank setdown, Alex very nearly tripped over his own feet. On second thought, this was worse than dancing with a general's wife at his first military ball. Then he could only be court-martialed. With Jane, the stakes were much higher.

He bowed and swung her lightly into the middle of the room. The few other dancers moved to the sides. It was reminiscent of the first and only other time they danced together, a time never very far from his mind. Only yesterday he had bought Jane's birthday present at Tessier's, a delicate porcelain music box with a couple performing a wild country dance.

"London may have been cruel to you in some ways, my dear Jane, but you will never go unnoticed or unappreciated again," he said, etching her face and her body into his mind for the cold future facing him.

They danced in perfect harmony, and he smiled down on her, willing her to put an end to his unhappiness. The music was about to end, and he needed to get away before he dragged her into a side room and kissed her and loved her into submission. It was an appealing thought, but he couldn't do it. He was, he decided, not the same unthinking, unfeeling Alex Barrington of Lady Bellingham's party. What a pity. He had lost the desire to be outrageous. What a terrible thing, to love without hope.

"I could wish London had been kinder to you, given you the glory you craved, fulfilled all you came to London for, but I can't," he said, gently pushing Jane away as far as his arms could reach. He wasn't going to beg. She knew his heart.

Jane felt suddenly abandoned, terrified. She said the first thing that came to her mind.

"I will be your mistress any time you come to Ireland."

Alex threw back his head and laughed derisively, causing everyone in the room to rivet on them again.

"No, thank you, I've had that," he said, his mouth grim, his manner cold. "You aren't the only one who has undergone an epiphany," he said, his hands gripping hers. "I don't know why, but since our nights in the studio, I want you, no one else, and I want all of it—wife, children, possessions. Yes, even miniatures and portraits for my children and my children's children down through the ages. For the first time in my life, I want to be like everyone else. I have stopped fighting myself. I recommend you do the same."

He stopped in the middle of the dance floor, while the musicians continued to play.

"I am the head of my family, and I shall assume the role I ran from with the same love and vigor I gave the British Army. I owe you much for opening my eyes. Take a chance with me. All the way."

"I can't be all you want. I wasn't born to be a grand chatelaine, to preside at country fetes and open garden parties. I can't."

Alex touched her cheek and signaled her suitors to take his place.

"You'd make a terrible mistress, Jane Daitry," he whispered, "but a wonderful wife. Good-bye."

Chapter Thirty-nine

Jane made her twice-daily pilgrimage to the huge black-and-white marble star in the center of the double entry hall at Dairy Hall. She was home, but not at home anymore.

It was one of the few traditions of old she could still observe and know a measure of pleasant memory. All the rest, her room now repainted, repapered, was alien. Long and consoling walks through the parkland and pastures of her childhood, when she would run away from her parents' battles, were for a simpler time and a simpler Jane Dairy.

She extended her arms, a solitary child again, pivoting above the star until her senses reeled. She opened her eyes to feast on the four unobstructed views of gardens, woodlands, parkland, and Craig Bay.

"Would you believe I missed seeing you of a morning, spinning about and painting for hours," Verna said gently, her hands resting on her belly, big with the child she and Patrick were expecting in a few months. It wasn't the same without you with your painting box drawing everything and everyone all day. You didn't know it, but I saved all the pictures you did of me and Patrick."

Jane laughed at the world of difference between the Verna she thought she knew and a Verna at last fulfilled. Kinder and more content, now that there was enough money for Patrick to bring the place to the state it had been before Thomas Dairy had succeeded to the title, she now regarded her sister-in-law with fondness.

Jane went to the chest in the hall and picked up a stack of freshly laundered linens, once a major bane between them. She bent and kissed Verna, who was now glowing with health and happiness. The pudding face was leaner, the eyes brighter, face unmarred. More and more Verna behaved like a lady to the manor born.

Verna's eyes followed Jane out of the hall. She called out to her.

"Will you never paint again, Jane?" Of course, Patrick cautioned her not to upset Jane, and she had promised. But it was past three months since Jane's return from London, and she had been quiet long enough. Some old habits died harder than others. I'd like to cover a wall in our bedroom as a record of the babe's progress."

"I honestly don't know about painting anymore," Jane replied. "Let me think on it."

She wanted to say that painting was far behind her, but there was time before the baby's birth. Indeed, she'd managed far sooner than she had expected to feel the hurts of the past fade with each day at home. The big stumbling block was what to do with herself all day and a good bit of the night. The country was too quiet; the hours stretched endlessly every blessed day, her hands idle, scrubbed clean a half-dozen times a day, as if to wash away a stubborn stain. She threw herself into the running of the house, and, to her amusement, found she was becoming a first-rate housekeeper.

And how much could she walk when she had no reason or desire to stop and sketch a budding flower, a horse galloping in the high meadow, the changing light of morning on the stable slates, the planes of a milkmaid's face at evening time, the poignant look of a tenant's wife nursing her baby?

What am I going to do with the rest of my life, she moaned in killing anguish in the quiet of her room? It was in this mood of loss and ennui that she was arranging the linens in the airing cupboard, and felt someone standing behind her.

"Aunt Madge has a visitor," Patrick said, resting on his sticks. "She thought you ought to know. He's leaving tomorrow."

Jane smoothed the scalloped edges of a lovely French pillow slip she had brought back as a gift for Verna.

"It's Alex," Patrick said, taking out his pipe and making a ceremony of reaming the bowl. "Madge asked me to tell you."

"I know," Jane said, worrying her lower lip. "I caught a glimpse of him at the horse sales the other day. Has he come to see how you are spending his money?"

"I wish I'd never told you about the loan. Janey, I know he offered for you. I got that out of Madge the week after you came home. You looked like death, and I had to know the reason," her brother said, squeezing her shoulder. "Can't you love him? Is he too overpowering for you, or is it that goddamned painting that's made you so unhappy all your life? Did that come between you?"

Until that moment, Patrick had taken care not to harry her either, and she was grateful to him.

"Did I make a mistake sending you to bloody London?" He asked as he pulled her against his coat.

"I told you and Aunt Madge it was too late for me to be all I wanted to be, but I went anyway. I could have stayed on here."

"Do you want to see Alex?"

"No. It wouldn't be fair. I'm burned to a cinder, and he will feel he has to do something to help me. I've taken enough of his charity," she said, smoothing the lapel of his fine new hacking jacket. Money in the bank, future fatherhood, and the first signs of a glorious future for the estate were working wonders for her brother, too. If only her difficulties could be settled so easily.

"I think you're a damn fool, but I won't force you," Patrick said sadly.

Later Jane went to her room and stood at the window, willing Alex to come riding over the brow of the hill. He wouldn't, and she wasn't sure it would be the answer to the nothingness that was the content of her life. She prowled the room, all manner of memories she thought she had excised beginning to plague her.

She was standing before the armoire in her room, when Lizzie came in.

"Take out the black-and-white riding costume, and please have Lightning saddled for me."

Lizzie left, and Jane held the costume close to her. Looking in the mirror, she remembered the day in Hyde Park just before Clea Wesley had found her and Alex and had helped her on the downhill road to where she was today. She no longer blamed Clea or Claude Morgan. The seeds of her desolation were hers alone. She had looked too high and fell too low to blame anyone but herself.

A half-hour later, horse and rider tore out of the cobbled stable yard and made for the hill behind the house, a short cut Jane had taken all her life to Madge Brooks's house. She gave the horse leave to eat up the miles, and within sight of the square Georgian mansion she pulled the horse and herself up short.

What am I doing? Alex has been here for a week, and never came near me, she sobbed, laying her cheek against the silken mane. *Why does it hurt so much? Will I never be in peace?*

"Now that's a picture," a voice said, coming up beside her on a quiet and surefooted hack. "You look almost human now that the wind has put some color in your cheeks, much better than looking like the last rose." Alex grinned, reaching for the bridle. "You should ride more often."

"Just like you to spy on me," Jane hooted back, pulling the reins out of his hands.

"Get down from that horse," Alex commanded, leaning over her saddle again. "I'm going to kiss some life into you."

She was stunned. But before she could regain her balance, Alex was off his horse and pulling her down to the grass. He slapped the horses' rumps and slid down beside her, knocking her hat sideways. He freed her ebony hair and spread it over her shoulders like a fan.

He leveled himself over her, his hardness hot against her. His hands were everywhere, exploring, caressing her breasts beneath the superfine jacket, his lips cool and his breath hot as he forced open her mouth.

"By heaven, you make me crazy." He laughed triumphantly, his pewter eyes smiling down on her. "Don't fight me."

His tongue was like an adder darting and teasing her until she cried out for release and opened her mouth and pulled him down on top of her. They kissed with a hunger that blazed and grew.

"You devil." Alex gloated. "You did come to me after all."

Jane cried out and bucked under him. "Go away."

It was a mistake.

Alex stopped at once, held his hands in midair, and turned over, his head rolling from side to side in the grass.

"Claude Morgan was right. Manley and I went to his house after you left to tear him limb from limb. The poor sod told us you were the kind destined to be inconsolable, with your vaulting, unattainable ambitions," he said, pounding his fists into the ground. "He's seen plenty of your kind. I'd feel sorry for you, if I didn't feel sorry for Madge and Patrick more. They think they should have left you to die here with all your illusions intact. James Manley thinks he failed you, and I feel like a damn fool for loving you."

"Can you make me a great artist?" Jane shouted at him. "Can you, or anyone, make me feel, make me want, make me whole again? I am lost, and no one can help me, if I can't help myself."

"I don't know how, but I will find the way," Alex whispered hoarsely and swept her into his arms.

Jane struggled against him.

"Is this how you will help me? Kiss away my little female hurts, my little disappointments? Alex, I'm dead inside. Can't you understand? I thought you knew how much I wanted to be something, someone. Oh, Alex, I was nothing for so long, and I wanted to be special."

"You are someone. Remember when you said you were completely alive when you painted? Go back to it. The hell with success. Please yourself. I know I can help you, gentle you," Alex said, making one last effort to find a way to reach her. "I can't tell you how, or if I can ever make up for your loss, but I want to be with you and hold you when the demons make you unhappy. I want to be there when you are in despair like this. I have no magic formula, except how I feel about you. Let me try."

"How easy it is to be glib," she said, ridiculing his plea.

He sat up and brushed the grass off his breeches and gave Jane his hand as he whistled for the horses grazing nearby.

"You have lost your reason to be," he said gravely, handing her the reins. "I know what that's like. But there is a time to mourn and there is a time to live. I think there's a verse for that in the Bible. I am trying to live, but you are the only phantom still haunting my life."

Alex touched his hat and watched Jane move toward her horse. He called after her.

"Run away again, Jane. You are very good at running away," he said bitterly. "Poor fool. I've waited thirty-five years to fall in love, but only you could have made me happy. Only you."

Jane woke with a cry, her white linen nightdress riding above her legs, the room an oven. She got out of bed and went to the window, slipping to the floor to wait for the dawn and escape from her endless nightmares.

The scene at the dinner table the night before with Verna and Patrick in ceaseless arguments about the estate mixed with the painful parting from Alex forced Jane to search within herself as never before. Indeed, the exercise took on a nightmare quality that had driven Jane to her bed.

She could no longer find ease in the house that had been her refuge all her life. Even the star in the center of the hall, the once-comforting vistas seen through the long windows surrounding the house held no charm for her.

It was time she faced the truth, Jane told herself. Only in Alex's arms did she feel the first measure of surging life in months. Remembering Alex lying full-length upon her made her pulses soar again.

Jane looked out at the wall of silence and blackness beyond the window. *Must I live for the rest of my days chasing after shattered dreams, mourning for Alex and what might have been? Do I want to live without the promise of the love Alex has offered me?*

All the old reasons for and against marrying Alex as a way of escaping poverty and disillusionment rang wildly in her head like clashing cymbals. Over and over again in the dead and dreaded small hours, here and in London, she feared that everything that made life worthwhile had died within her, never to burn again.

Did she have anything left in her to give and receive love? After all, her work had been for so long the end and be-all of her existence. The specter of self-pity as a way of life was crushing to contemplate.

Jane never questioned her love for Alex, but she was afraid she would cheat him, living as she seemed with half a heart.

The litany of arguments that littered her life went on. *I won't cheat him. It isn't fair to offer myself as I am now. Alex deserves a whole woman, not a battered shadow.* Yet without Alex and her work, what would become of her? Could she live without Alex and the glimpse of heaven he promised her so often and so assuredly? *If he has faith in his power to help heal me, should I not have faith and believe in him and myself?*

At once Jane rose from the floor, took a small branch of candles, and flew down the stairs to the library in search of the family Bible. Could Alex's salvation from his own terrible disappointment be hers as well?

Her fingers skimmed wildly until she found what she was looking for. She closed the Bible, retrieved the candles, and made her way upstairs.

With trembling fingers she turned the handle of a door and was assailed by an oppressive odor of old paint and stale air. It was the first time since she had returned that she dared brave the room that had been her studio, the scene of years of hope, despair, and doubt that she now knew all artists were heir to.

She raised the candles and made a slow circuit of the room, a retrospective of another time and a different Jane Daitry. Blinded by ambition beyond her limited talents, she knew she had lost her way and forgotten the simple joys and promises of creating pictures. She no longer needed nor wanted the praise of the Clea Wesleys and Claude Morgans of the world. She did not have to paint for anyone but herself.

The words of *Ecclesiastes* she found in the Bible showed her the way:

> To everything there is a season,
> And a time to every purpose under the
> heaven . . .
> A time to weep, and a time to laugh;
> A time to mourn, and a time to dance.

Jane laughed exultantly and left the room.

Alex watched the thick, blue smoke of his chcroot spiral into the darkened ceiling, as dressed for travel, he lay in Madge Brook's best guest room on the second floor of the sprawling old house. An overwhelming sense of loss swept over him. He was going to spend the rest of his life miserable without Jane because he couldn't breach the wall she had built around herself.

He was leaving at dawn, and was too sick at heart to do more than count the hours. He put out the cigar and turned his head into the pillow.

Sometime later, Madge's dogs set up a wail. At the same moment he heard a horse circling the front of the house, spraying cinders, disturbing the night air.

A string of pebbles rained against the windows, and Alex bolted out of bed. Below he saw a woman in a filmy white night rail dancing in the coming dawn.

"I *can* make you happy, Alex," Jane called up to him, throwing her arms wide.

Alex vaulted down the stairs three at a time, and flung back the door.

Jane was laughing and crying and hurled herself into his arms.

"Come dance with me, and I *will* make you happy. Now!"